DEAD DRUNK II

Richard Johnson

*This is a work of fiction. Names, characters, businesses, places,
events and incidents are either the products of the author's
imagination or used in a fictitious manner. Any resemblance to
actual persons, living or dead, or actual events is purely
coincidental.*

Author webpage www.facebook.com/RichardJohnsonDeadDrunk
Cover Illustration Copyright © 2014 by Richard Johnson
Cover design by Derek Murphy of CreativINDIECovers
Copyediting by www.ManuscriptMagic.com

Chapter 1
The Lost Boys

"I don't care how many times you say it, Grace Jones was not, I repeat, *not* a fucking Bond Girl," Charlie Campbell said as he struggled to put one aching foot in front of the other.

"She's in the credits dude," Left-Nut replied. "Plus, she was pretty nasty in Vamp. Her red wig and whiteface scared the crap out of me and gave me major chub when I was a kid."

The group plodded through yet another patch of timber. Six hours of walking and it was the same pattern over and over – walk through a section of the woods, sprint through a field, rest and repeat. The light-hearted conversations, dumb as they were, kept their minds off the terrors of the day and the monotony of their hike.

Charlie cracked a smile. "The scariest thing in that movie was her Adam's apple. And I wouldn't bang her with your baby-dick. I'm really starting to question your standards."

Left-Nut clicked his tongue. "I told you guys, standards are like expiration dates. Close your eyes and they don't exist."

Smokey pointed to Left-Nut's white hair, which had recently gotten much whiter during the course of their escape from the city. "It's a good thing you don't have standards 'cause you aren't going to be pulling any kind of chicks now, you Obi-Wan Kenobi-looking son of a bitch."

"We can pick him up some Just For Men Gel," Rob said, uncharacteristically jumping into the fray. "No play for Mr. Gray."

Left-Nut stopped walking as they entered a clearing. "It ain't so bad. You can call me the silver fox, baby. Anyways, are we even going in the right direction? This field looks familiar."

The plan had been to follow the power lines through the countryside, but when the lines veered into a city that appeared to have been consumed by flames and a massive bombardment of artillery, an audible was called for.

Big Rob nodded. "Pretty sure I know how to go straight west. Just follow the setting sun. Duh."

"Okay, fine. So I guess that isn't the same tree I pissed on an hour ago?" Left-Nut pointed to a massive oak tree that had the word "boner" crudely written on it in yellow liquid.

"Damn it, and here I thought you knew what you were talking about for once," Charlie said to Rob through gritted teeth.

Rob sighed. "The sun was overhead for a bit, so I couldn't see which direction—"

"Way to go, Bear Grylls," Left-Nut interrupted and instinctively backed up.

Charlie took charge and had the group turn thirty degrees to their left. Moments later they sprinted across the unpicked bean field for the second time. Charlie and Left-Nut arrived first and waited in the shade for the slower members of the party.

The friends had survived a zombie outbreak, starvation, bad luck, a touch of madness, a Chinese military invasion and a hell-ride out of Chicago. Now everything hinged on their outdoor skills and teamwork. In other words, they were screwed.

"Look, I realize nobody wants to say it, but that was a huge fuck up," Left-Nut said between heavy breaths. "We can't be adding any extra miles now that we're on foot."

"Yeah, and what's your point?" Charlie asked.

"No more decisions from Rob, and I mean *none*. The guy is a walking calamity."

Charlie shook his head. "At least he's stepping up. You haven't done a thing but bitch this entire time. As a matter of fact, even Zombie Cliff was a bigger help than you back at the apartment."

"I just saved us from walking in circles, didn't I? And on top of that—"

As if on cue, a zombie shot out from between the tall plants nearby and grabbed Left-Nut from behind, cutting his foul tirade short. Left-Nut somehow managed to twist free and fell farther into the weeds while Charlie scrambled to pick up his Chinese assault rifle. But rather than press the attack, the zombie merely stood in place, pawing in the direction of its intended victim.

Left-Nut rose to his feet and peered cautiously at the beast's expressionless face. The man had once been a retired game warden, spending his golden years angling for steelhead and king salmon. Now he was a glorified digestive system.

Left-Nut grinned as the others ran up, their weapons at the ready. "Haha, this dumb-shit's stuck in a bear trap. I was about to karate chop the crap out of him and then teabag—"

"*KACHINK!*"

"Aughhh!" Left-Nut screamed as he stepped onto a second bear trap hidden in the grass and the 38-pound snapper locked tight.

At that moment the zombie's shredded foot tore loose from his own contraption, and he lumbered forward once more. The zombie fisherman didn't get far – after a few steps, the front of his head burst apart and splattered all over a screaming Left-Nut.

But the gunfire hadn't come from Charlie's crew, and it didn't stop with the demise of the solitary cannibal. "Get

9

down!" Charlie called as more bullets whistled past them and tore through the tree branches.

The crew scurried behind trees for cover while Left-Nut screamed in agony and fruitlessly yanked at the steel device buried deep into his shin. Luckily for him – though he was not feeling so lucky at the moment – the trap was heavily rusted and not working properly. Its weaker grip saved him from an even more grievous wound.

The firing stopped and Charlie peeked around his tree, spotting two people in tan uniforms about forty yards away. They were busy reloading their rifles, so Charlie rose to shoot in their general direction, hoping to drive them off with the automatic fire. He did even better than that.

Now two people were screaming, one in pain and one with grief. Charlie and Smokey ran towards the newcomers while Rob attempted to pry the trap open using nothing but brute strength.

A hysterical man knelt over his fallen friend, oblivious to the approach of Charlie and Smokey. They quickly gathered the men's rifles and peered deeper into the forest.

"Is there anyone else out there?" Smokey asked the standing stranger as Charlie sat down to check on the other. The young man shook his head and then buried his face into his hands again.

Charlie rolled the motionless man onto his stomach and found a gaping exit wound in the center of his back. On an impulse he tried to plug the hole with his hands, but he realized it was pointless. The lifeblood had already drained from his body, leaving behind a puzzled expression frozen on the young man's gentle face.

It was at that point that Charlie got a better look at the uniforms, and his heart sank. They were Boy Scouts.

Chapter 2
Finger Lickin' Good

Russ casually threw a metal trashcan through the door of a darkened gas station and walked in without hesitation. For whatever reason, be it his scent, the way he breathed, or some other unknown mechanism, the zombies flat-out ignored him now and he was basically free to go about his business unhindered. His business for now was finding some whiskey, and any whiskey would do.

Trent, however, had no such special abilities and was on edge while waiting nearby on his freshly pilfered motorcycle. The naked woman painted on the side was supposed to be Angelina Jolie, but the artist had bitten off more than he could chew, and his attempt had resulted in the woman looking more like Sandra Bernhard.

Eventually he could wait no more and snuck inside to see just what in the bloody hell was taking so long. Not surprisingly, he found Russ in the liquor aisle. "I thought you had to take a dump?"

"I did. That cop I ate went right through me. Indian food always does," Russ said, then took a heavy gulp from a fifth of room-temperature Jack Daniels. He coughed heavily. "Smooth."

"She wasn't *Indian* Indian, she was Native American. But whatever. Fucking idiot." Trent's newfound religiosity had been short lived, with Russ's shenanigans pushing him back to his natural position of chaotic neutrality with a hint of dickishness thrown in for good measure.

The dynamic duo had realized riding through Chicago was too dangerous by day, and had wisely holed up in an appliance store until midnight. Their second attempt to flee the city had been just five minutes underway when Russ pulled the surprise pit stop.

"You just drank a whole bottle while we were hiding out and you're already drunk again? Seriously, you got a problem. And that means something coming from me."

Russ capped his whiskey and then offered up a water bottle to the third member of "Bad Company." Elvis the raccoon grabbed the bottle in his nimble hands and drank heartily. "Thirsty devil," Russ said, then made his way to the beef jerky. "Hell yeah, teriyaki." He took a huge bite of trucker steak but immediately spit it out like poison. "Damn."

"I didn't think jerky could spoil," Trent said.

"It doesn't, but ever since I got bitten everything tastes like shit. Except for your partner. She was finger-lickin' good. And I'm starting to get hungry again." Russ walked towards Trent. "We're talking ravenous." The stab wound on Russ's arm was bleeding onto the floor and he remained completely unaware of it.

Trent backed up and moved his scabbed finger to the trigger of his holstered pistol. This was the situation he'd been dreading since Russ rescued him that morning. He appreciated the liberation, but if he had to put Russ down he would do it without hesitation. He might even enjoy it.

Russ saw the fear in the cop's eyes. "Now hold on there, Tinker Bell. That's what the whiskey's for."

"Bullshit. You want me to believe it's a cure?"

Russ chuckled, but his unblinking eyes made the gesture anything but reassuring. "No, but if you haven't noticed, I'm kind of an alcoholic. And when I drink, eating never crosses my mind. Unless I'm at a strip joint, if you catch my drift. In that case, line me up at the buffet."

"I guess that makes sense." Trent relaxed and then chased some painkillers with a warm beer from a six-pack on the floor. He let out a quiet belch and rubbed Elvis's head before draining the rest of the beer in one long pull.

The raccoon made a strange purring type noise and then wandered over to eat Russ's discarded jerky.

"Suppose we better get back to it." Russ picked up Elvis after he had eaten his fill and walked towards the door. "Same plan, right? Gonna keep heading north for a bit and then shoot west to try and meet up with the gang?"

Trent nodded and grabbed some sour cream potato chips, then stuffed two more beers into his pockets for the ride. "This is gonna be a killer booze cruise."

"Yep," Russ said. He grabbed a pair of cheap sunglasses for himself and a child's pair for Elvis, then went to check for any nearby stragglers outside. After a moment he waved Trent over.

They climbed aboard their respective choppers and took off, alternating between cluttered roads and sidewalks, depending on the obstacles.

Soon they had left their old neighborhood, and the zombie population began to pick up dramatically. Even worse, the savages they passed along the way were now swarming behind them, unable to keep up but following just the same. But Russ and Trent rode past the bulk of them with little effort, and there had been no sign of the Chinese invaders.

The easy ride came to an abrupt halt as they spotted an overturned semi ahead that completely blocked their route. Russ took the lead and turned west down a side street only to find a crumbled apartment building that was partially on fire. The crowd of zombies was getting closer as the pair circled back and headed east, then south.

Then things really got shitty. Machine gun fire from a Chinese patrol up ahead drove them away, and so they headed west once more. Luckily the shooting drew the zombie crowd's attention and sent them smack dab into the Chinese position. An initial hail of gunfire ended abruptly as the soldiers were overwhelmed, demonstrating once more the unpredictability of biological weapons.

The motorcycles approached a foreboding landmark several miles later – Richard Daley Prison – and with it came an unsettling sight. Just outside the new prison's double barbwire fence, three wooden crosses had been pounded into the ground at various heights with men attached to each one. Duct tape was wrapped around the men's limbs dozens of times, creating an unbreakable seal.

Below them was a handful of zombies in various states of injury. Some were missing limbs or horribly burned, but all circled like hungry sharks waiting for a chance to strike.

One of the tied up men had been set lower than the others which resulted in his feet getting gnawed off by the crowd. He'd obviously gone zombie and now strained to look at the other two motionless captives.

"Sucks to be them," Russ said and prepared to ride off again.

"Should we do something?" Trent asked, hoping Russ would say no.

"I suppose I could eat the sumbitches. They're tied up for a reason. Must be murderers or animal rapists or something."

Trent nodded in agreement, but an unknown force tugged at his heartstrings, begging him to act. It was his much-neglected conscience returning from a decade-long hiatus. He was feeling guilty about abandoning his partner, and also remorse for murdering a man on the day of the outbreak. The die was cast as Trent cut his engine. "Screw it... let's cut 'em down."

"Okey dokey," Russ said with a shrug. Trent was still a turd, but at least he was trying. For now.

*　　　　　*　　　　　*

Marquell Washington raised his battered head as the motorcycles approached, wondering who the newcomers might be. Not that it mattered to him. For the second time in months, the ruthless gang leader was waiting to die. This time Marquell had been blindsided by the woman he'd left in charge of the prison. During his brief absence she had led a rebellion, which resulted in one heck of a breakup.

Of course, he *had* murdered her husband, the warden, and the relationship had been far from consensual. So he should have seen the double cross coming from miles away, but amazing breasts have a way of clouding a man's thoughts, even one as brilliant as Marquell.

For her part, Heather McCabe had taken the prison with the help of loyal guards and a surprise attack, striking when Marquell left to get medicine for her sick dog. Now she slept peacefully for the first time in months, snuggled up with the poor dog she'd poisoned herself and dreaming about mani-pedis and iced coffees.

The crucifixion was simply Heather's homage to Marquell's fiendish peculiarities. She didn't have the historical knowledge of torture that he possessed, and so this was her best go of it. Still, it wasn't a bad message to keep outsiders from coming too close.

Marquell wasn't alone in his predicament. Two surviving lieutenants initially joined him in the live performance art, but only one of them remained. Mad-Dawg Mike's cross was shorter than the others, and so his feet were promptly devoured by the crowd below. Marquell's other henchman, Ace Kool, was still conscious, but a bullet hole in his shoulder was taking its toll and he was fading fast.

Marquell could see the two men arguing in the distance and it looked like they might leave. So he raised his dreadlocked head and called out for help, driving the zombies at his feet into a frenzy. Even worse, he risked alerting the guard in the nearby tower. The feared marksman and turncoat only known as Gus was eager to shoot Marquell, and would do so without hesitation if he attempted escape.

Every zombie and human below the tower would have been easy targets for Gus, but he was currently jamming to electronica through his headphones while getting a sub-par blowjob from one of the prison nurses. Being second in command had its privileges, and for helping Heather with her dangerous plot, his rewards had come quickly indeed.

As one of the men dismounted from his motorcycle, Ace managed a whisper. "Whatever happens, don't leave me, Markee. I'm not ready for the Big Sleep."

"That ain't happening, Ace. We always and forever, blood for life," Marquell replied. But following the motto of The Black Lords might be impossible under the circumstances, and for Marquell, self-preservation was much stronger than brotherhood.

Defying all logic and common sense, the man dressed like a pirate walked towards the crowd of zombies carrying a mere crowbar. In moments the beasts would be upon him and the stranger would add to their ranks as just one more hungry mouth.

Only it didn't quite work out that way.

"What the..." Marquell's words trailed off as the crowbar clanged against a zombie's forehead and flew from the man's hand, sticking into the dirt. But the zombie ignored both the attack and the man, and still focused intently on Ace's feet.

"The name's Russ and I'll have you boys down in a jiffy," the man said. He picked up the iron bar, smashing it into the zombie's face and killing it this time. Blood oozed off the crowbar as he looked at Marquell with eyes deadish and empty. "That is, as long as you're not kiddie-diddlers or lawyers. You're not, are ya?"

"No man," Marquell managed to sputter out through his disbelief. Russ nodded and continued the slaughter of

16

the defenseless zombies, a task made more difficult by the fact that he really sucked at it. The 'slaughter' consisted of Russ slipping in blood, falling down, and missing his targets all while cursing heartily.

"Watch this one Trent, I'm like Bobby Bonilla over here." A swing and a miss. He paused to take a drink from a brown bottle, and it became clear to Marquell just what was going on. Russ was shitfaced.

Trent rolled his eyes at his idiotic antics and walked closer as Russ finished off the last of the infected. But then he recognized Marquell, and his hair stood on end. The muscle-bound man in the middle was the leader of the raiders they'd scuffled with the day before.

How the man had ended up in his current predicament was unclear, but Trent instantly questioned his own call. He thought about leaving them behind to their fate, but the memory of shooting an innocent man was weighing him down, and if rescuing a couple scumbags could lighten the load he would do it. Not to mention, Trent couldn't shake the feeling he was being tested by a higher power.

He climbed the cross and used his pocketknife to sever Marquell's polyethylene bonds, then tossed the knife to Russ before jumping to the ground.

Russ scaled the second cross while Trent gave Marquell a stoic look. "Don't try anything funny. We're gonna cut your buddy down and then you two are on your own."

Marquell nodded. "That's straight. I'm Marquell, he's Ace."

"How'd you end up out here anyways?" Trent asked, arching a suspicious eyebrow.

"Bitches, man, you know how it is."

"Yeah, I sure do." Trent rubbed his sore jaw with sliced up hands, compliments of his own female problems. "You guys should—"

"Auuugh! Auuugh, ughh—" Ace Kool screamed in pain and then stopped abruptly as Russ severed his vocal cords with a nasty bite. His body went limp briefly and then reanimated, but the heroin dealer was now but a shadow of his former self.

Russ clung to the man in an awkward embrace while a vein dangled between a gap in his front teeth, dribbling out hot crimson blood. The drunk looked more like an entrant in a wing-eating contest than a ravenous beast, but for a moment, that's just what he was. "Juicy," Russ said as he licked his fingers.

Chapter 3
Creeper

Charlie closed the dead child's eyes and turned to the other boy, who was now rolling on the ground in hysterics. Left-Nut was screaming bloody murder even louder in the distance.

"Shut him up, quick," Charlie said while patting the anguished scout's shoulder.

The kid paused his whimpering when Charlie spoke to him softly. "Buddy, please take it down a notch. He's gone."

"No crap, you killed him. He was the one friend I had left. Now I'm all alone."

"What were you thinking, shooting at us for no reason? I thought it was the Chinese again, so of course we were gonna shoot back."

"He thought you were the monsters and started firing, and I just kinda followed him. That's what I always did."

Charlie sighed and changed tactics. "Look, what's your name, partner?"

"Sam. My name's Sam. And you're not my partner." The boy pointed to the dead body. "He was."

"I promise, we won't hurt you. Believe it or not, we're the good guys," Charlie said and looked towards Left-Nut, who was still screaming every curse word known to man. "Sort of."

Sam sat up and wiped the last tear from his eyes. "We'll see."

Left-Nut continued to yell, and by now the noise was drawing in random zombies from across the field.

"I said shut him up!" Charlie whisper-shouted at Rob once more.

Big Rob's beefy fist slammed into Left-Nut's jaw and knocked him out effortlessly. "Night night," he said and calmly grabbed his baseball bat with the bent handle. The zombies running towards him from the bean field were soon met with a trio of headshots. A school nurse, yoga instructor, and tax lawyer all went down in an instant. The gentle giant finished the poor nurse off with a coup de grace and fought the urge to vomit as he wiped the brains off his weapon. At least the killing part was getting easier.

Charlie looked to the kid and struggled for the right tone of voice to use. "I'll prove that you can trust us. You can have your gun back as soon as you calm down." He nodded at the fallen scout. "What was his name?"

"Colin. He was the troop leader's son."

"Was it just you two out here?" Smokey asked, not wanting any surprises.

"There were eight of us at first. We were camping out when everything happened and, and..."

"That's fine, little dude," Smokey said. "We'll talk about it later."

Charlie nodded. "Yeah, we better get moving. Need to find a place to hide out and treat Left-Nut's leg."

"Left-Nut?" Sam asked.

"Umm, Matt's his real name," Charlie said. "He got stuck in a bear trap over there."

Sam nodded. "Colin's dad was using those to catch the creepers. He went into Biggsburg a few weeks ago and never came back."

"Is that the town right across the way?" Charlie asked.

"Yeah, it's where we all lived."

"It looked pretty messed up," Smokey said, and Sam started crying again. "But we were just on the outskirts, so it's hard to tell," he added hastily and unconvincingly. "Was your family there? I mean, *is* your family there?"

"No, I'm a foster kid. I don't care what happened to my foster family. The scouts were the only people who gave a damn about me."

Charlie looked at the freckle-faced boy and struggled to maintain his own composure. The kid had already been alone his whole life, and now this turd sandwich of an apocalypse had been thrust into his face.

"Sam, I'm a good judge of character, and I'm looking at you and seeing a dude that's about five foot tall and maybe a hundred pounds soaking wet. Your stats on paper aren't real good, but the fact you're even alive at this point leads me to believe you're a total badass." Sam wiped away his tears and stood up a little taller as Charlie continued, "Now, what just happened here was messed up, but it was an accident. So you can either dwell on it or you can move forward and join our crew. Since you've made it this far, I'm betting I know your answer."

Sam smiled slightly, which was amazing given the circumstances. "Yeah, I guess I don't have much of a choice. What about Colin though?" he asked as Smokey handed the rifle back to him, an old .22 Sam had earned a merit badge with by shooting tin cans.

"There's nothing we can do for him, but we need to get going," Charlie said. "How close is your camp, and is there anything useful there? Supplies, food?"

"About a quarter mile into the woods, but it's bare. We used up pretty much everything. I've got about ten bullets left in my pocket. That's why we were out here hunting rabbits."

"Gotcha," Charlie said as the group rejoined Big Rob and Left-Nut.

After introductions were made they settled on a new route. Sam had told them that nothing useful lay west for miles, and since the city was off limits they decided to see what was to the north. Rob slung Left-Nut over his shoulder like a sack of defective Christmas presents, and

21

their already slow pace trickled to a crawl. Losing the four wheelers earlier in the day now appeared to be an even bigger disaster, and Charlie reminded Smokey of this fact numerous times.

The next hour was a boring slog as the group traversed yet more fields and wooded areas, as well as a few much-appreciated pastures. They were no longer able to run across open areas, and if a Chinese patrol caught them in a clearing it would be a massacre.

Through a little prodding from Smokey, Sam told them of his months in the woods, and it was a rather depressing tale. His group lost two members on the day of the outbreak as they came in from the woods, gunned down by a panicking sheriff's department. Down to six people, several more died a week later, gobbled up as they slept in their tents. Running low on supplies, another scout was shot while approaching a farmhouse he thought was abandoned.

After that fiasco, the scout leader kept them in the heart of the woods and scavenged for supplies by himself. One day he never came back, and Sam and Colin were on their own, left scared, hungry, and confused.

"The tent incident was horrible. The kids were screaming one second and attacking us the next. Colin's dad, Frank, built a platform onto a tree stand the next day and then the creepers couldn't find us."

"A tent's a bad idea, it's just a sandwich wrapper as far as I'm concerned," Smokey said. "You call them creepers?"

"Yeah. It's because they're all quiet and they just creep up on you."

"Makes sense, but we just call 'em zombies. The infected kind, mind you – the undead ones are a whole different ball of wax," Smokey added, always one to show off his knowledge on the subject matter.

"The biggest creeper you'll meet is this guy right there," Charlie said and pointed at Left-Nut.

"Why's that?" Sam asked.

"Just wait until he wakes up, you'll see," Rob said and shook his passed out friend gently for emphasis, causing blood to ooze from his injured leg. "Whoops. He did go out like a light, though. Talk about a one-punch pussy."

"Damn, that's a lot of blood. We gotta find somewhere to get him cleaned up," Charlie said, and then a sinking feeling came over him. "Sam, did you say your scout leader was using those traps to catch the creepers or zombies or whatever the hell you want to call them?"

"Yeah."

Charlie frowned. "I hope Left-Nut didn't catch the infection. Getting caught in that bloody trap would have to be like sharing a needle."

"It doesn't work like that. We've been covered in blood and nothing happened. Shit, Rob's practically bathed in the stuff," Smokey said. "It's all about the bites. I'd say something in the saliva spreads the infection."

"Just keep an eye out. If he starts acting funny, drop him on the ground and back up quick."

The walk to nowhere in particular continued, and it was Sam who struck up the conversation this time. "If we're going to be travelling together, why don't you tell me a little about you guys and where we're headed?"

"Fair enough. I'm a teacher—"

"Substitute," Smokey cut in.

"I'm a *substitute* teacher, Smokey's a pothead, Rob's a fighter and Left-Nut's a psychopath. Big Rob, Lefty and myself grew up together, and we met Smokey in college."

"It's cool that you're with old friends."

Charlie continued, "We were living in Chicago, and like you, our original group was much bigger... we left the city and now we're trying to meet up with my girlfriend and some others at a military base by Cantonville."

"Sounds plausible," Sam said. He didn't entirely trust his new companions due to the circumstances, and the fact that nobody in his life had been worth trusting so far. Plus, being abandoned as a toddler and getting shipped

23

around to five foster homes had left deep emotional scars. Seeing his friends eaten alive hadn't helped.

"Since we don't have the four wheelers we started on, thanks to Smokey, I'm sure you'll know everything about us within a few days. Perhaps more than you care to."

Charlie stopped talking as they exited a particularly thick patch of woods and came upon a clearing. A hundred yards out was a stone building complex surrounded by a blacked-out chain-link privacy fence. No roads or sidewalks led to the odd structure that resembled a Spanish presidio. It just looked plain out of place.

The men cautiously approached the main gate with Sam crouched behind them, taking no chances. Charlie pointed to a small sign by the locked entrance and read it aloud. "Poor Sisters of the Cross Convent. No trespassing, no solicitors, no visitors. Violators will be prayed for on site."

"That's a relief, I thought maybe Count Chocula lived here," Smokey said with a snicker. "Man, do I miss cereal."

There was no movement around the compound, so Charlie scaled the fence and opened the gate from the inside. Next was a quick jaunt to the main building that left them all totally exposed. A man with a rifle could have taken them down with little effort.

However, no such man was waiting, and moments later Charlie knocked on the front door as the others looked around for signs of life. Twisted gargoyle statues leered down at them from above and all the windows had been painted black. The place was as quiet as a cemetery, and a well-kept vegetable garden was the only hint that it was occupied.

Charlie took a few short breaths and opened the steel door, finding a locked wooden door behind it. He knocked on the small viewing window and backed up, his finger on the trigger of his Chinese assault rifle.

Nobody answered, so he knocked much louder the

second time. He looked to Smokey and whispered, "Why don't you run around the place and check for more doors." Smokey took off, but just as Charlie turned back, a nun appeared in the window, startling the bejesus out of him. The woman wore a white coif and a traditional brown habit, looking like something straight from the 1800s. And she was drop-dead gorgeous.

"Whoa, you kinda snuck up on me there," Charlie said while trying to regain his composure. The nun stared quietly for an awkward minute and then turned her head, revealing a massive, bubbly scar that covered the entire left side of her face. "Fucking zombie!" Charlie gasped and prepared to blast the woman through the door.

"Whoa dude, chill!" Smokey shouted as he reappeared with an elderly nun close behind him.

The old nun gave Charlie a look that could have melted his own face off. "Put down the toy gun, you probably scared Sister Katya half to death. Now just what is going on? This gentleman informed me that someone is injured?"

Charlie pointed to his unconscious friend. "He got his leg stuck in a bear trap."

"Oh my," the nun said and raised a hand to her mouth. "You'd better get him to the hospital in Biggsburg. I'm afraid we have very limited resources here."

"Lady, um, I don't think tha—"

"Not lady, my name is Mother Agnes Vukavka, and I'm the Mother Superior of this small order. By the way, you gentlemen are trespassing. And Halloween isn't for a few weeks so I am a bit confused by your outfits."

Dressed like a comic book hero, a cowboy, a Boy Scout, a 70s porn star, and a rather convincing drug-dealer, they did look like a strange offshoot of the Village People. But Charlie focused on the most important aspect of the conversation. "Lady – I mean, Mother Superior, we can't just stroll into town and go to prompt care."

"I suppose you don't have insurance?"

"Wait, what? No, it's not that. Seriously, don't you know what kinda shit-storm hit us these past couple months?"

The nun took a step away from the men. "This is all a bit confusing, and frankly you people are putting off some bad vibes. Are you on drugs or something?"

"Dang, I wish," Smokey said under his breath.

"You're telling me you don't know about the zombies?" Charlie said.

"What in the world is a zompy?" the nun asked, now thinking she was dealing with conmen at best and criminals at worst. "I think I should call the sheriff and he can sort this out." Of course, this was a bluff as she had no phone.

Charlie lost his cool. "Sheriff? There's no freaking sheriff left! There aren't any cops, no hospitals, no churches, no schools, nothing, it's all gone!"

Rob tapped Charlie's shoulder. "Calm down, bro."

"Now are you gonna open this door or do I have to kick the damn thing in?"

"This conversation is over, gentlemen. Please leave."

Charlie refused to take no for an answer and ran at the front door, kicking it as hard as he could, and failing spectacularly. "Son of a bitch," he said with a groan and fell to the ground, rubbing his throbbing foot. To his credit, the door had a slight scuff mark on it.

The yelling had not gone unnoticed, and a nightmarishly disfigured man emerged from the forest and quickly made its way to the fence. Here it found the gate still partially open, thanks to Smokey being the last one to enter.

As the gate clanged against the fence and the zombie lurched onward, all eyes turned to the incoming abomination. It had wandered the forest for months, having been plagued by stinging insects, thorns, curious coyotes, and the summer elements. Now the hungry creature was nearly unrecognizable as a human. Its skin tight from dehydration and its eyes shrunken, the zombie locked in on a target and charged. Mother Agnes stood frozen in both fear and disbelief as it closed in.

Rob fumbled with his bat, then accidentally kicked it away as he reached to pick it up. Charlie and Smokey raised their guns but didn't have enough time to shoot. The zombie hammered the nun to the ground and opened its festering mouth wide. A split second later it was dead, felled by a rifle bullet through the eye socket.

Sam walked over and pulled the twitching creature off the nun. Up close, it smelled even worse than it looked. The infected man shuddered once before ultimately escaping the purgatory he'd been trapped in, and a state of peace appeared on his withered husk of a face.

"There's your *zompy* right there, lady," Charlie said.

Rob ruffled Sam's shaggy brown hair. "Nice shooting, Tex."

"That's the first one I actually hit," he said, beaming with pride.

The Mother Superior rose from the ground and smoothed out her clothing before taking a deep breath.

"He's the priest from town. Now I know why he never bothered showing up for his annual summer visit."

"Sorry," Charlie said.

"He was a blowhard." Mother Agnes pointed to Left-Nut, still comatose, as her godly vows finally kicked in. "Let's get the injured one inside and see what we can do. We are healers, after all."

The disfigured and barefoot nun opened the door from the inside and greeted her much older superior with a nod. Oddly enough, the woman didn't say anything about the deadly encounter she'd just witnessed, but her eyes were a mile wide.

"You just can't come in past the entryway. This is a cloistered convent." The men looked at her as if she were speaking Aramaic. "It means we don't allow visitors. This is a quiet place of prayer, reflective thought, repentance, and most importantly, solitude."

Of course, it was at that moment Left-Nut woke up from his punch-induced slumber.

"Ouch, my fucking leg! And where's that horse-cock motherfucker Rob at? That shithead sucker punched me in the god-damned mouth. I'm gonna blow his stupid nuts off!" He caught a glimpse of the scarred nun's good side and his disposition changed instantly. "Ooh, hello."

Charlie looked at Sam. "See, I told you. Total creeper."

Chapter 4
Three Amigos

Russ chewed happily on Ace's warm flesh before shaking his head like a man waking up from a vivid nightmare. "Aw shit, what did I just do?"

"You ate my friend, that's what you did," Marquell said, puffing up but not getting too loud in the process. He was unwilling to let his anger alert the nearby sharpshooter, though it didn't really matter right now. Said sharpshooter was about to have his first orgasm in months and wasn't worried about their plight in the least bit.

Russ bowed his head and pointed to a bullet wound on the expired man's gut. "I just couldn't help myself. Must be a side effect or whatnot. He was gonna die anyways though, honest."

Trent whistled at them both and pointed to the horde of zombies charging up the road. "We'll sort this out later, but we gotta go. Marquell, you can either come with us or climb back up on that cross. Your pick."

"Fine, but I'm not riding with that crazy motherfucker. Did you see what he just did?"

Russ climbed down while sucking the blood off his fingers like sticky syrup. "I'm not hungry now, brother, I just ate."

"See? Dude's crazy. No, I'm riding with you," Marquell said and walked next to Trent, keeping a wary eye on Russ the entire time.

"Climb aboard then, cupcake," Trent said and brushed the seat off behind him as if cleaning it for a girlfriend.

With no time to spare they fired up their motorcycles and took off, all thinking about different things. Trent was seriously questioning his decision to stop, Marquell was trying to calm himself down, and Russ was wondering if he could reach the bottle of whiskey behind him without crashing his chopper.

Soon their thinking converged to one topic, and it was where in the hell should they go next. More roadblocks, fires, and the growing army of cannibals rapidly cut down their options.

The two motorcycles pulled up next to each other and Trent turned to Marquell. "I'm stumped. How well do you know the city?"

"Like nobody else. I used to own these streets. We need to head three blocks north, and then two west."

"I'm listening, but then what?" Trent asked while Russ took advantage of the brief pause in action to scratch Elvis's head and take a swig of the brown stuff as a palate cleanser. The raccoon cooed with pleasure and pushed its body farther into Russ's four-fingered hand. Zombie Cliff had eaten the missing digit the day before, but it hadn't seemed to slow the man down much.

"There's an old steel mill right there with a TARP entrance inside. I had some underlings making meth for me in the tunnels there."

"TARP tunnels?" Trent asked. "Never heard of 'em."

"Water drainage tunnels. Damn deep and thirty feet wide. We can take them all the way out of the city. No muss, no fuss."

"I hope you know what you're talking about. Russ, come on."

In a few minutes, the trio pulled up to the mill and parked their motorcycles by the front door. The change in plans was a big one, and Trent was hesitant about listening to their new "friend." But they simply had no other options. The next dead end would have been a literal one, and the cop started panicking on the inside.

They shut the door behind them and entered a long, empty hallway. Trent turned on his police-issued Maglite and led the way while Marquell kept a safe distance from Russ. He was still fuming about the ignominious end to his friend's life, and once the trio came into the plant cafeteria, Marquell stopped.

"Before we go any farther, y'all have some explaining to do. Like, what's going on with that peckerwood right there?"

"Russ is... a little under the weather," Trent said.

"That's what you sick bastards call it? Look, you better be one hundred with me. No bull, and I'm not playing."

"He's infected, sort of," Trent said. "Not like the dumb-fucks running around eating people. I guess he's still a dumb-fuck running around eating people, but not like the other ones. He can talk."

"Gee, thanks for your kind words," Russ mumbled, proving that, indeed, zombies can have feelings.

"Anyways, we think he might be the cure to ending this whole thing, like in the movies. So we're trying to find scientists or a military base or whatever." Marquell smirked and Trent lost it. "You got any better ideas, asshole? Least we're trying to come up with something."

"Your child-like interpretations of communicable diseases are a joke and your escape plan was dog shit too. Couple of simpletons." Marquell was stirring the pot deliberately now to test their mettle and gage their response. The master manipulator could usually get others to react precisely as he wanted.

Trent took the bait and his temperature started rising. "A little gratitude would be nice." He moved a hand to his holstered weapon. "We did cut you down. You were just zombie bait without us."

"Lordy, Lordy, thank you, thank you. If I'm lucky, someday I'll get to come in from the fields on a rainy day and mend your shoes by the campfire. Maybe even sing some hymns."

"Typical," the cop said dryly. Old habits die hard, especially for jerk-wads like Trent

"What's that supposed to mean?" Marquell said and grinned on the inside. It hadn't taken him long to find the man's weakness.

"Just what I said, typical. Your kind are always unthankful. We should have picked our own damned cotton five hundred years ago. Ain't that right, Russ?"

Marquell snorted. "Your historical knowledge is dog shit too. And I was the one behind bars? Talk about an unjust society."

"That was a good home for you. How about we take you back? That's right, back to where somebody beat your ass and tied you up like a chocolate sacrifice to King Kong."

"Oh, I'm done with that place," Marquell said. "And don't think I didn't recognize you from yesterday. You're the buster that boned out when shit was getting real. Left your friends to fend for themselves. You served and protected the hell out of them, didn't you?"

Trent was speechless for the first time in a while and Russ finally jumped in.

"Both of you need to cut the crap. Elvis and I are sick of listening to it." Russ punctuated this point by taking a slug of whiskey. "And frankly, I'm getting bored."

"Fine, let's hear your masterful escape plan, Marquell," Trent said, eager to change the subject. "Like with these tunnels, are they gonna be full of water and crap? Did you think that through, genius?"

"No man, the tunnels aren't fully connected to the system yet so they should be empty still. One hundred plus miles of concrete tunnels. We're only going twenty, though."

"And how do you know about this shit anyways?" Trent said.

"Bored," Russ interjected with a huff.

"This was my planned escape route from prison if I ever got the chance," Marquell said, then paused. "I guess I did get the chance. Anyway, should be maps all along the walls down there and safety stations with emergency food, water and flashlights. I had my cookers scouting the place out for me. Bunch of idiots, but they made me money."

"Not bad," Trent said, feeling like he'd made the right decision after all. "But what happens when we leave the tunnel?"

"See, that's where my plan really takes shape. We pop out and find a vehicle, then drive to a small airport not too far from the city. I had some pilots who were junkies, and they made runs for me so they could wet their beaks. I bet one of those planes is still there, and I know where the keys are. We grab it and fly to wherever we damned want. Oh, and there might be some meth left behind in the tunnels, too. Can use that for barter along the way."

Trent's eyes widened and his teeth clenched slightly at the mention of the drugs, and Marquell saw the cop's other major weakness. This would be easier than he thought.

"I take it you can fly?" Trent asked as they entered yet another empty room, finding countless cobwebs and storage lockers. The smell of mildew was thick and the air felt dirty.

"Never have, but I could play flight simulator when I was high on some dank-ass weed. The real thing can't be much harder. It's just pitch control, banking, power control and shit like that."

"And landing," Russ added, becoming the unlikely voice of reason.

"I find your lack of motherfuckin' faith disturbing."

A smile crossed the trucker's lips that was off putting when paired with his vacant eyes. "Hey, that's from *Star Wars*. Are you a fan?"

Marquell grinned back, showing off the charming side he could produce at will – the hallmark of a true psychopath. "You damn right. Baron Lando Calrissian was a pimp. If that shit was real, though, he'd a turned Princess Leia out in a minute."

"God, I thought I was done with the dumbass conversations," Trent said with a groan. "Let's move."

"Not as long as I'm around," Russ said. "Marquell, you kinda remind me of a young Eddie Murphy, before the tranny incident. Not judging him, mind you, I had my own run-ins with a few over the years when I hauled gravel for a living. You gotta, and I repeat, *gotta* check for the Adam's apple. That's always a dead giveaway."

"Eddie Murphy? What decade do you think this is? You achy breaky vampire motherfucker—"

"Zombie," Russ corrected him emphatically, very proud of his affliction.

Marquell shut his mouth and followed them farther into the maze of rooms, content to put up with their insults and ridiculous actions for now. He'd gain their trust, learn their idiosyncrasies, and even entertain them if he had to. But when the time was right, Marquell would kill them without a second thought.

Chapter 5
Girls' Night Out

Cindy hung up her phone and looked at the other girls in the bachelorette party with a bemused expression on her lovely face. "Jim just told me they're at a pizza place right now. The funny thing is I could hear the distinct sounds of a strip club in the background. I could almost smell the cotton candy perfume."

Jen, the bachelorette and Blake's fiancée, took out her own phone. "Yeah, he's full of shit. Watch this," she said and placed a call of her own, taking a drink of her umpteenth martini as she let it ring.

In the midst of getting a lap dance at The Sugar Shack, Blake picked up and did his best impression of a bored, sober guy. "Yeah, we're at a taco place at the moment, getting ready to turn in after we grab some nachos. It's been a pretty lame night." In the background, someone shouted obscenities in broken English. Something about Cheetos and boobs.

"Sounds kind of loud for a taco place," Jen said.

"It's one of those late night—"

There was a fumbling sound over the phone and a man with a thick accent got on. "I have a hairy balls." It was Vidu. Drunk, horny, angry, and a bit confused. Just a normal Friday night.

Jen rolled her eyes and hung up, not realizing it would be the last time she ever talked to her fiancé. "Yeah, they're totally at a strip club."

The group of women had enjoyed their own wild night of partying and recently returned to Jen's condo to wind down. Still, it hadn't been completely wild. Lots of flirting, some sitting on laps, a few makeout sessions, but not the pants-crapping insane bender the guys were currently having.

"You don't seem that pissed. I'm fuming over here," Cindy said as she fought the urge to call her husband again. The pregnant fitness instructor was the sole sober one of the group and was currently thinking up numerous ways to make Jim miserable over his indiscretions. Withholding sex was always an old standby. Minimal effort, maximum payback.

Jen shrugged. "Boys will be boys."

Jackie, Jen's maid of honor, came in from the kitchen with a freshly opened bottle of red wine. "If I catch Bruce up to no good I'll send his pasty butt packing in a heartbeat. Once that business starts, it never stops." The Southside native and daughter of a former congressman had an authoritative air about her, and what she said was definitely not a bluff. "But who goes out for hotdogs when you have steak at home? Am I right ladies?" she said and grabbed her own breasts for emphasis.

"I'll try a bit of that steak," said Kelly, another friend, and tried to grab a boob, only to have Jackie playfully slap her hand away. Kelly was one-half of the identical twins known affectionately as the "Nut and the Slut." She was the slut. By a mile. Her sister Monica had already passed out in a spare bedroom after downing too many shots of tequila. The poor girl never even made it to the bar and was now sleeping with her high heels on and a gum wrapper stuck to her forehead.

"Seriously though, and I mean no offense, but Blake's college friends are losers," Jackie said. "Why does he even hang out with those guys?" She received an instant dirty look from Cindy. Her husband was one of those losers.

"It's one of those situations where he feels stuck with them. But to be honest, he won't be seeing most of them after the wedding. I'll see to that. They're holding him

36

back." She looked to Cindy. "Not Jim, of course. He's solid as a rock."

Now it was Padma's turn to speak. She was Jen's college roommate, a great friend, and even better trauma surgeon. "Blake's friends are lame, but is it true what they say about Big Rob?"

"What about him?" Jen said.

"That he's hung like John Dillinger?"

"I have no idea what that means, but you have my full attention," Kelly said and Jen shrugged as well.

"There was a story in our anatomy class about John Dillinger... you know, the famous bank robber? Anyways, there was a rumor that he was so big he had to have his pants specially tailored to fit his enormous junk. Supposedly after the cops killed him right here in Chicago, historians pickled the old pickle – for posterity, I'm sure. Other rumors say it's still floating around the Smithsonian somewhere."

Jen nodded. "I'm pretty sure it's true. Rob's about the size of Shaquille O'Neal, so if he's just proportionate... but the guy's a total teddy bear and kind of a simpleton, so he probably wouldn't know what to do with it anyway."

"I can show him," Kelly said with an impish grin. "But speaking of Blake's friends, weren't you going to set Padma up with that Vidu guy?" The dark-skinned beauty threw a pillow at Kelly and she almost spilled her beer.

"Watch it, hookers. You spill, you pay," Jen said and eyed her white carpet for any damage.

Padma was not finished. "Just because I'm Indian doesn't mean I'd date that guy because he's Sri Lankan. Not to mention he's a complete moron. I only met him briefly, but I'd swear that guy is inbred. Besides—"

The conversation was interrupted by the loud buzz of the intercom system. "Miko's delivery," came the voice on the other end.

"Awesome, it's the Greek I ordered," Jen said and buzzed him up. "Sorry, but the penis cake you guys bought wasn't cutting it for me." She answered the door a minute later and let the man inside. "Just put it on the counter."

The short and tan deliveryman set a large paper sack down and smiled heartily, looking like he'd come directly from the Jersey Shore.

"Oh, this guy looks legit," Padma said.

At that moment the man ripped his detachable pants off lightning quick and pushed play on the boom box disguised as takeout. "Did somebody order kielbasa?"

Cindy's mouth shot open in disbelief as the stripper's sweatpants hit the floor. "Are you serious?"

"Girls will be girls," Jen said and finished her martini with a monster gulp as Kelly turned the volume up on the boom box.

The fast-moving Greek stripper wasted no time, and the aptly named Magic Miko was like a force of nature. He could pop it and lock it, do The Dougie, pelvic thrust like no other, and his rendition of The Running Man was priceless. And of course, there was his patented finishing move, The Wrecking Balls. Big Rob had been right earlier in the night after all because the bachelorette party did indeed have a big dong waving in their collective faces. And they loved every fake-tanned, spastic, oily second of it too.

After a fifteen-minute performance that was worth every dollar paid in advance – as well as every bill shoved down Miko's leopard thong – the group of friends found themselves ready to turn in for the night... except for Kelly, who decided kissing strangers at the bar wasn't the most embarrassing thing she could accomplish that evening. She moved her unconscious sister to the floor and waited for the ravishing promised by the smooth talking entertainer.

Meanwhile, Miko paced in the bathroom after downing a bottle of Pepto-Bismol he had pilfered from the medicine cabinet. His stomach began aching during the show and his smiling face hid the sheer terror he felt inside, as he worried about dropping a deuce in front of the cheering women.

"Get your sexy ass in here you little Mediterranean mango," Kelly said from the guest bedroom and slapped her pillow for emphasis. The skinny brunette was ready for action, but at the same time starting to fall asleep.

Niko splashed cold water on his sweating face as the churning in his stomach stopped. "You can do this," he said and began popping generic boner pills like breath mints. The steroid-addicted supercharged sex addict had forced himself on a passed out Asian woman on the train just minutes earlier, so the little pills were necessary to rise to the occasion on such short notice. Still, the girl waiting for him in the bedroom was hot, and Niko was quite sure her twin sister would want to get in on the action too. He planned to cop a feel at the minimum even if she wasn't. Niko gave a predatory smile into the mirror and winked. It was show time once more.

*   *   *

The next morning Jen sipped black coffee in her living room and dialed Blake for the tenth time. It went straight to voicemail, leading Jen to believe she was intentionally being avoided. She was.

Cindy had the same luck getting through to Jim. "They're either passed out or some girls are over there," she said and walked around in the kitchen still cluttered with empty bottles of various types.

Jackie chased an aspirin with a gulp of orange juice and rubbed her eyes. "Relax, you don't need to be stressing out in your condition. And besides, there's a man over here too if you haven't forgotten."

"How could I forget? I could hear those two going at it all night. Talk about a skank. And her sister was in the room, which is a total faux pas."

"Yeah, that's pretty embarrassing, even for her. But we should get Mr. Banana Hammock out of here in case the guys show up unexpectedly," Jen said. "I'd rather not have to explain what he was doing here." She walked upstairs and knocked softly on the bedroom door.

Magic Miko's little pills had eventually kicked in, and he had given Kelly quite a night to remember. Unfortunately, she didn't remember any of it. Even worse, the sweaty, snoring man lying next to her had been passing gas that smelled more than a little like gyros.

The tapping at the door and the noxious smell was enough to drive her to action, and she slid out from underneath his hairy arm and got dressed. A moment later, she woke her sister and retreated downstairs in what amounted to a very short walk of shame.

Standing in the doorway, Jen tried unsuccessfully to rouse the dancer from the bed. In response, Miko groaned in pain and then whimpered softly before growing quiet.

"I'll get him out," Cindy said and sauntered over with a smug look on her face. She was eager to harp on her husband later and didn't want this guy to weaken her hand. "Time to go, buddy," she said with the conviction of a woman used to being obeyed. There was no response from the smoothly shaved dancer. "Hey, Miko, wake up and hit the bricks!" Cindy turned to her friends while fanning the air. "It smells like crap and tzatziki sauce in there. Really, Miko, you gotta get out before—"

The man suddenly jumped up and shot through the doorway and slammed into Cindy, causing both of them to tumble down the stairs before crashing into the wall with a thud. The impact was hard enough to knock a row of pictures to the ground, and it happened so fast everyone did a double take before reacting. But when

40

Miko began feasting on Cindy's neck, react they did. Mostly by screaming.

The twins and Padma ran outside while Jen sprinted around Miko as he munched on Cindy like a juicy watermelon. Miko caught the movement from the corner of his eye and turned to snag Jen's leg, taking her down with a tug from his chiseled stripper arms. Those buff arms had always put food on the table, and they would continue to do so in zombie form.

But one of the women wasn't screaming or running in terror, and before Miko tore into Jen's leg, Jackie smashed a full bottle of red wine square into his face. The blunt impact rocked him backwards as the spray of blood and wine drenched Jen's beloved white carpeting.

Next, Jackie grabbed an unresponsive Cindy by the arm and dragged her towards the open front door. No longer stunned, Miko rose up and gave chase, but he moved with a strange gait, as if running was a newly acquired skill. Jen swung the door shut behind her just as Miko slammed into it from the opposite side.

To their surprise he didn't open the door, and instead battered it with his fists. None of Jen's neighbors answered her frantic calls for help, and the other girls were nowhere to be seen. So Jackie and Jen dragged Cindy outside – and smack-dab into the apocalypse.

The apartment building across the road had just gone up in flames and cars whipped by at dangerous speeds. Padma and the twins tried to flag down help, but nobody would stop. Soon a large group of 5k runners came down the street at a very fast pace — only it was two groups, and one was chasing the other.

Padma used a tampon from her purse to plug Cindy's gaping neck wound, and the girls huddled around each other for comfort as the world they knew evaporated before their eyes. For the moment, standing still seemed to work as the cannibals passed them up for the moving prey.

At long last, a squad car pulled up and a cop jumped out with his gun drawn. The tall man approached the women cautiously while swiveling his head in all directions. Before he could even say anything, another man from the running group veered from the pack and charged right for him. The sharp crack of a pistol rang out and the runner dropped to his knees, then fell face first onto the pavement. There was a giant exit hole on the back of his head and blood quickly formed a dark puddle on the ground.

The cop kicked the dead body once for good measure and then pointed to his cruiser. "Get in the damned car, ladies. As you can see we have a bit of a situation developing."

There was no hesitation from the twins and they jumped right into the back seat, but the others stopped to pick Cindy up. "I got her," the cop said and pushed them aside, then wrapped his arms around the woman's pregnant waist from behind. He was handsome, confident, commanding, and just the kind of guy you'd want around in a pinch. He turned to Jackie with a roguish smile and winked. "Everything's gonna be all right."

Cindy opened her eyes and turned to him, and it looked like she was going to say thanks. Instead, Jim's wife latched onto the cop's wrist with a vicious bite, severing tendons and bones with ease. He screamed in pain and his damaged nerves caused the gun to fire off uselessly into the distance. A moment later he turned on the women with the same bloodthirsty look on his face that first Miko and now Cindy wore. Everything was not all right. Far from it. In fact, everything sucked.

But before he could pounce on them, another woman ran up to the group in a panic. "Help me officer, help me!"

The cop did the exact opposite of help, and instead knocked her down and bit into the barista's exposed stomach. Cindy joined in and pulled the poor woman's gleaming intestines out before jamming the grayish organ

42

into her mouth. Inside Cindy's womb, her zombified baby kicked with anticipation for the meal headed its way.

The random woman's demise, as grisly as it was, saved Jen and company from the same fate, and they had just enough time to pile into the front seat of the car. As Jackie hit the gas, the zombie cop, Cindy, and the mutilated woman all pounded on the windows, eager for the fresh meat inside.

Jackie drove away and the women finally had a chance to catch their breath for a moment. But they all had the same thought on their minds.

"Where do we go?" Kelly asked from the back seat.

"There's a police station a couple blocks away," Jackie said and swerved around several creatures feasting on a midget in the middle of the road. "That's our best bet."

Moments later they arrived at the station, and were immediately let down. The front door was shattered and a large group of cannibals was streaming inside. They were met with gunfire and several fell, but more just kept coming, and soon the firing stopped. Jackie took her foot off the brake and moved on as her friends either sobbed or sat stone-faced and silent.

"We can try and meet up with Blake and his friends. They're not too far away," Jen said as she tried to call her fiancé unsuccessfully one more time.

Jackie shook her head. "They might be dead by now. My father's yacht is at Belmont Harbor and it's a straight shot from here. We'll be safer out on the open water."

"I wouldn't be so sure," Padma said. "We could—"

The surgeon's words were interrupted by Kelly puking violently onto the bulletproof window separating the front seat from the back of the car.

"She's not looking so good," Monica said, stating the painfully obvious as the brownish liquid cascaded onto the floor. The convulsions came next.

"That's not a hangover," Padma said ominously. "Was she bitten or something?"

"How am I supposed to know?" Monica said and grasped at the door handle, but she was unable to unlock it from the inside. "Guys, open it! Like, now!" Her sister started licking her lips and drooling like an idiot.

"I'm working on it," Jackie said and began frantically pushing buttons on the dashboard. Unfortunately, one of them turned the sirens on and a large group of beasts instantly made a beeline for the car. Soon they were surrounded and had to stop as the mob beat on the doors and windows, threatening to burst in at a moment's notice. The doors finally unlocked, but now Monica had nowhere to go. She could only look at her twin sister and pray for a miracle.

Kelly stopped shaking and stared off into space as if watching her life flash before her eyes. In reality, most of her brain was shutting down and all of her memories and the moments she once cherished were disappearing forever.

The car shot forward, then Jackie slammed on the brakes and hit reverse, knocking some creatures down and gaining momentum in the process. She repeated the maneuver and gained even more speed while smashing a handful of hungry attackers. Bones crunched, limbs snapped and blood flowed. If they could free themselves of the crowd though, Monica could jump out to safety and join them in the front seat.

Padma held a hand to the glass divider and touched Monica's, praying with her longtime friend. They made eye contact just as Kelly snapped out of her trance and turned to her sister for sustenance.

Monica grabbed Kelly by her throat and held the snapping jaws at bay. It wasn't the first time she'd choked her sister, and oddly, the situation made her recall other fights the two had gotten into throughout the years including spats over toys, bunk beds, and of course, boys. But their whole lives had been completely entwined from the beginning; they had shared an egg after all. And so, even with their occasional quarrels, Monica could not imagine life any other way.

"No, don't!" Padma shouted, but it was too late. Monica embraced her sister in one final hug and screamed in pain as Kelly went to work.

Thankfully the sounds of the siren shielded the other women from the noises of the feast, and after a few seconds, it was all over. Jackie slammed on the gas once more and broke free of the pack, powering down the road with dozens, if not hundreds of zombies, trailing behind.

"We're gonna have to time this just right," she said while barely avoiding runners and crashed vehicles. "The boat's at the end of the pier, so there's a bit of a run. I'll work on getting it started, Padma's gonna untie the ropes, and Jen, grab one of the oars from the dingy and keep any bastards from jumping on. Are we all clear?" They were. "No mistakes."

The twins began pounding on the divider in unison, reunited in purpose once more and sharing the same hunger for flesh. Jen snuck a peek at her infected friends and began to crack under the pressure. "What is happening? This is madness."

"Turn around and get your game face on," Jackie said with a determined look of her own. "Let's worry about the why later." Jen nodded and took a deep breath.

Her pep talk over, Jackie slowed down and approached a busy intersection as cars whizzed past them from all sides. A woman in the middle of the road used the brief reduction in speed to her advantage and jumped onto the back of the car. She began pounding heavily on the roof, and the added mayhem of the situation was about to push even Jackie over the edge.

But soon the marina was in sight, and Jackie spotted her family's boat. She drove as close to the docks as possible and then slammed on the brakes, sending the woman on the roof flying into the drink at high speed. At the same time, Kelly and Monica's heads smashed into

45

the hard divider and they left the world as they came into it. Bloody, but together.

Jen, Padma and Jackie exited the car and got busy doing their assigned tasks. Jackie found the hidden spare key and fired up the engine while Padma struggled to untie the first of the knots holding the boat to the dock.

Meanwhile, Jen prowled back and forth on the deck of the yacht, looking for anyone who needed bashing. She quickly found her first target when the woman from the roof of the car swam to shore and then tried to jump into the boat. Jen swung and connected with the woman's stomach, knocking her to the floor.

"Ouch, what was that for?" the woman screamed as she rolled over and sat up. "Are you crazy?"

"I thought you were one of the maniacs!" Jen said, still gripping the oar and preparing to strike again.

She shook her head. "No! I was just trying to get away from those... things. The grocery store I work at was on fire and everyone was going mad. I saw the police car and jumped on. You didn't hear me screaming for the past five minutes?"

Jen lowered her bludgeon slightly. "The siren was on, so no, we—"

She stopped as a giant of a man came running down the dock and barreled onto the boat with murder on his mind. What was left of it, anyway. The former head of security for Belmont Harbor was still chewing a mouthful of belly flesh from his previous victim, but he clamored for more. And Jen was already in his grasp. She brought the oar up and caught the man underneath his chin while Padma stopped what she was doing to help.

But the zombie weathered the blow from Jen's stick and ignored Padma's well-placed kick to the groin. He swallowed the chunk of meat already in his mouth and leaned forward to replace it with a fresh one. At the last moment the grocery girl jumped on his back, and all three tipped over with a crash.

Padma furiously kicked at the security guard's head as the other women tried to scramble away. He merely rolled onto his back and grabbed Padma's foot, opening his mouth wide once again.

There was a loud pop and a bright light as the guard's head suddenly radiated sparks, accompanied by smoke, and a sickly burning smell not easily described. Jackie had fired a 12-gauge flare gun into the gaping maw of their attacker, and the burning round had burrowed all the way through to his brain.

Jackie undid the last knotted rope with several deft maneuvers then silently walked back to the helm of the boat. She had known Jake the security guard since childhood.

Padma helped Jen shove the dead body into the water and then nodded to the stranger. "I'm Padma, that's Jen and Jackie."

The new arrival sat down and began rubbing her stomach again. "Mary."

Jackie pulled the boat away as more zombies jumped off the pier, only to sink below the choppy waters of Lake Michigan. No one spoke as they left the doomed city behind for good, but they were all thinking about their next step. It was the end of the world as they knew it, and nobody felt fine.

Chapter 6
Breaking Bread

The nun with the disfigured face went to retrieve bandages for Left-Nut's wound, and the aforementioned jerk got a better look at her. "Yikes! Talk about a butterface. She's got a body built for porn but a face made for radio."

Charlie gritted his teeth and narrowly avoided lashing out. "Left-Nut – I mean, Matt – shut it. We're guests here."

"Not saying I wouldn't hit it," Left-Nut continued. "Because you know I'd hit it like a baby seal. The nuns back when I was a—"

"Rob, knock him out again," Charlie said.

"Fine, fine. Look, I'm in a lot of pain right now. I need something to take the edge off, so is anyone holding? Smokey, I'm looking strongly in your direction."

The mother superior was shocked and appalled, but kept her mouth shut given the circumstances. A zombie had just attacked her, after all. That kind of life experience tends to expand one's mind no matter who you are.

Smokey hemmed and hawed but eventually gave in. "I wanted to save this for a special occasion but I guess this will do." He pulled a prescription bottle from the front of his underwear.

"Why not use your pocket?" Sam asked.

"Old habits are hard to break. But still, here's some hillbilly heroin. That's OxyContin for you squares," Smokey said proudly.

"I'd suck his dick if it had morphine in it," Left-Nut said. "Now hand it over, chop chop."

"My boy Julio used to get this for me by the case. Lincoln Park cougars loved the stuff. Chew the pills up and they'll affect you faster, but they taste like crap, bro." Smokey looked at the nun. "I mean... poop." The guys were really struggling to regulate their vocabulary after months of living like animals. Not that they had been much better before the zombie apocalypse.

Left-Nut took a handful of the brown tablets and chased them with the last drops of Big Rob's flask, taking down the piss-warm rum with gusto. Fifteen minutes later he was in a lot less pain and totally blistered. After several nuns cleaned and dressed his wound, Charlie and Rob put him in an empty bedroom to rest.

"I'm gonna discipline the monkey and take a nap. Best pain killer there is," Left-Nut said.

Charlie closed the door without responding, and then the guys took the rare opportunity to clean themselves up. They walked to another spare room already supplied with buckets of hot water, sponges, and homemade soap. Charlie savored the indulgence as much as he could and then retired to a surprisingly comfortable couch to catch some winks. The safer surroundings, his clean skin, and the peaceful ambiance of the convent put him to sleep in less than a minute. It didn't last.

"La, lalalalalala, la la!" Rob belted out opera in the bathroom while vigorously scrubbing the zombie splatter from his body. The bucket turned red as bits and pieces of flesh bobbed up and down in the water. "Figaro, Figaro, Figaro!"

Charlie put a pillow over his head, but the noise actually seemed to get louder. However, the annoyance was soon forgotten as one of his other senses went into overdrive. The smell of freshly baked bread filled the room, and Charlie's mouth watered like never before. A home cooked meal would be a thing of beauty after weeks of cat food and beef jerky. He knocked on the bathroom door. "Hey, Enrico Pullazo, hurry up in there. They're ready to serve lunch."

Rob heard the magic words and grabbed a towel in an instant. He was still dripping wet when he came out a few seconds later with soap bubbles still clinging to his beard. "I think I smell it."

They met Sam and Smokey in the hallway and made their way towards the dining area. Charlie noticed skylights in every room, and there were no visible lamps or light switches. "They don't have electricity."

"Doesn't matter to me as long as the food's good," Rob noted as they entered the dining room. About a dozen elderly nuns joined them at a plain wooden table in the nondescript room. The scarred-up nun brought in a basket of piping-hot, freshly baked bread and pitchers of water.

"Smells great," Rob said and grabbed an entire loaf, shoving it into his cavernous mouth as the women stared at him in disbelief. The sounds he made could almost be described as sexual in nature.

"Um, Rob," Charlie said and gave him an elbow.

Rob continued to chew slowly until he noticed the glare from the Mother Superior. So he set the crusty loaf down, albeit under protest, and Agnes began to say a short prayer. Twenty minutes later she gave the signal that it was okay to eat.

Unfortunately, it turned out the bread was not an appetizer as Rob suspected, but the main course. When squash was brought in as dessert instead of the apple pie he had been imagining, it appeared Rob was about to have a major meltdown.

Seeing his friend in distress, Charlie gave Rob the rest of his own bread, thanked the nuns for the meal, and then addressed Mother Agnes with something that had been bothering him. "I gotta ask about something. You said you had no idea about the zombie situation before today, but you seem strangely stoic about the fact that a deranged priest just tried to eat you. I'm a bit confused."

Agnes Vukavka smiled at Charlie, but there was little warmth behind her expression. "If the dead are coming back to life it means that the return of Christ, our Savior, is at hand, and we have nothing to fear. This is what we have prepared for our whole lives."

"It ain't like that, trust me," Charlie said. "They're just sick people. They got chewed on and then they turned into cannibals. It's like rabies, and honestly, I don't think God has anything to do with it."

"I think you're wrong, young man. After all, this very scenario was written in Isaiah 26:19. But your dead will live; their bodies will rise. You who dwell in the dust, wake up and shout for joy."

Charlie bit his lip while trying not to lose his temper. They needed help and sanctuary, not bible lessons. Still, he had to make them see reality.

"That priest outside wasn't exactly shouting for joy when he tried to bite your face off. He was... well, trying to bite your face off."

Smokey gave Sam a high five. "Again, excellent shot, bro. Took him down like a boss." The preteen beamed with pride. Fitting in was something he'd never done, and his new acquaintances, as crazy as they were, seemed to be trying hard to bring him into the fold. To an orphan, that meant a lot.

The nuns were alarmed to see someone challenging their leader, but having taken an oath of silence, all they could do was look down in anticipation of the haranguing that was sure to come.

However, Agnes didn't respond with the anger they'd come to expect.

"You're right. I don't know precisely what's going on. But God's mysteries aren't always apparent to us, now are they?"

"I guess not," Charlie conceded with a sigh.

"I'm confident all will be revealed in good time, especially with plenty of prayer and introspection – which, by the way, is our specialty here."

"You work on figuring out God's mysteries and we'll work on fixing our friend up," Charlie said with a bit of sarcasm creeping into his voice.

Agnes nodded.

"Biggsburg is a small town about three miles away. A doctor's office there would have what you need. Tetanus shots, bandages, iodine. I wish we could help more, but we only use what we make ourselves."

"We passed it on our way here," Smokey said. "What's left of it. Unfortunately the place looked pretty toasted."

"I can lead you around the town," Sam said. "I know it pretty well and—"

"That's not happening," Charlie replied. "The place is a mess. Sorry, but you're staying here."

"You said I'm part of the group and now you're already kicking me out?"

Charlie quickly changed tactics. "No. Somebody has to stay behind and protect the convent from..." Charlie was going to say "Left-Nut," but realized that wouldn't sit well with his hosts. "The zombies. That's your job." He looked to Agnes. "Can you draw us a map?"

She nodded. "Yes. The office won't be hard to find."

"If the place hasn't burned down already," Smokey added.

The meal ended on that note, so Charlie and company went back to the spare rooms to get their gear. He longingly looked at the unadorned yet cozy room. Soft blankets and fresh, clean sheets were the types of simple pleasures that had become luxuries during the apocalypse. Plus, there were no giant rats lurking in the shadows, no rotting corpses festering outside, and no whiskey farts lingering around like an unwanted roommate. Leaving the convent so soon was the last thing

Charlie Campbell wanted to do. Especially for Left-Nut, of all people.

"I'll be honest, I don't want to go," Smokey said, vocalizing what Charlie was thinking. "Maybe we just leave Lefty here?"

But Rob would have none of it. "Without treatment he'll go downhill fast and probably die. Remember, we never leave a man behind. Even if he is an asshole."

Charlie nodded. "Rob's right. About the asshole part, mostly. Plus, if there is a God, I'm pretty sure he'd take a dump on us if we left Matt Tucker in a convent without adult supervision. That's just asking for it."

"Fine," Smokey said. "I'll go, but as long as we're shopping I'd like to pick up a little medicinal marijuana. For my glaucoma, of course."

"Of course," Charlie said. "We'd better have at it, though. The quicker we get there the quicker we get back and get rested up. Then we can go home. I can't wait to see Brooke and Brandon. And what's this I heard about Rob getting a kiss from Kate?" Rob's face reddened at the mention of it. "She sticks a knife in my neck and kisses you, huh? Nice."

With the banter done, the men geared up and stopped by to check on Left-Nut, who was being tended to by the younger nun that seemed to be everywhere. She was dabbing at his oozing wound while he made obnoxious gestures where she couldn't see.

"We're leaving to find you meds," Charlie said, not amused. "We'll be back in a few hours. I told that Sam kid to shoot you if you start acting up. I think he will."

"Can you refill my Viagra prescription while you're there?"

Charlie was even less amused. "I swear, the one difference between you and a bag of crap is the bag. Anyways, we don't have time to chitchat. We'll be back."

"Guys, thanks," Left-Nut said, dropping his shtick for once and surprising even himself. Then he smiled a toothy grin as the shapely nun started up with a sponge once more. "Soooo... tell me about your horribly disfigured face." He still had it.

*   *   *

Every step Charlie took through the forest pissed him off more than the one before. Here he was, risking his life for someone he almost threw to the zombies days earlier. Even worse, his goal of reuniting with his pregnant girlfriend was being put on the backburner indefinitely. Being the good guy was getting old fast.

Rob shook the forest with one of his signature farts and his eyes grew wide. "Woops. I should have held that one in a little longer to ripen."

"Damn, that's gonna itch when it dries," Smokey said.

Rob nodded. "Yeah, I better grab some leaves."

Charlie chuckled loudly at his friends and his mood improved considerably while Big Rob disappeared behind some foliage. Sometimes it helped to laugh at the ridiculous parts of life. With these guys there was plenty of material.

"Fellas, you're gonna want to see this," Rob said from the bushes.

"I highly doubt that," Charlie shot back. "Wipe your bunghole and let's go."

"No, I mean really, come check it out," Rob said with more urgency in his voice. Sure enough, he'd discovered a small clearing that held a gruesome discovery.

Smokey peeked around Rob. "Bummer."

In front of them was a mass grave with bodies in differing states of decay. The fallen residents of Biggsburg had been covered with quicklime in a failed attempt to dissolve the corpses. Some had faces frozen in terror with mouths open in silent screams, a testament to how horrible their final moments had been. Even creepier were the ones that looked like they might still be among the living, with eyes glistening and lifelike. One of those fresh bodies was wearing a Boy Scout uniform and knee-high socks. Charlie pointed to the man and sighed.

"It looks like Scout Leader Frank didn't make it after all. Should we tell Sam? Personally, I'd say—"

There was movement on the other side of the grave and the guys were forced to freeze in place to avoid being spotted.

Several weary Chinese soldiers came through the clearing, pushing wheelbarrows heavily laden with even more bodies. One soldier in green seemed to be supervising four other men dressed in slightly different brown uniforms. He barked an order and the soldiers tossed the bodies into the pit. The tangle of limbs and torsos, bloody stumps and burnt skin was as disgusting as it was tragic. Each body took with it a story never to be told, and represented a final insult for the poor souls consumed by a chain of events far removed from the little town in the middle of nowhere.

Their grim task finished, the leader shouted again and the men lined up on the edge of the pile, facing away from him. The stocky junior sergeant casually pulled his sidearm and fired into the back of one man's head. The body slumped to the ground before tipping forward into the abyss. A second shot rang out and another man dropped down with blood spurting in fits from his opened skull.

The sergeant aimed for the third man and pulled the trigger, but the weapon did not fire. He fiddled with it for a moment and then raised his weapon again. But this time, he dropped dead.

Without thinking of the consequences, Charlie had used up the last of his machine gun rounds with a sudden burst. It had been rather satisfying. The two remaining soldiers looked at him briefly, then disappeared into the woods, confused but happy to escape their summary execution.

Charlie and company waited for more soldiers to come streaming into the area to annihilate them, but none did. Soon the forest was quiet again except for the sound of blood trickling down the mountain of bodies. It was almost peaceful.

"What are the Chinese doing way out here? And why are they shooting each other?" Charlie asked while grabbing the officer's 5.8 mm pistol and ammo.

"Maybe food's getting low?" Rob said, proving once more what occupied most of his limited thinking power.

"Possibly," Smokey said, getting that familiar smug look on his face. "But the ones that just got shot weren't Chinese. They were wearing North Korean uniforms."

"How would you—"

"Gay Mike and I used to get baked and watch that shitty Red Dawn remake over and over. Between you and me, I think he had a thing for Chris Hemwsworth. But anyways, those brown uniforms look just like the ones the Norks wore in the movie."

Charlie took a last look at the dead and moved on, spatially and emotionally. "They must have disobeyed orders. Poor bastards are on their own now, though. Let's hope nobody comes looking for the other jerkwad."

They followed the tracks of the wheelbarrows out of the area and came upon an empty bean field. On the other side was the strip mall, exactly where Mother Agnes's map said it would be. It also became clear what the Chinese were up to in the area. Monstrous cooling towers loomed over the ruined town, billowing steam out like a pair of twin volcanoes.

"It's a nuke plant. Great. They're probably swarming all over the place to secure it," Charlie said. "Can't be having meltdowns getting in the way of their invasion, I suppose."

Rob started jogging across the field. "We're so close, can't turn back now. Just have this one little field to cross. Easy *peasy*," he added, making a rare joke.

"Those are beans," Charlie said. "But you're right. Make it quick."

A minute later they reached the back of the strip mall and used an access ladder to reach the roof. Smokey had theorized the door up top would have been propped open so workers could sneak cigarettes, and he was right. The guy was on a roll.

A stroll down the stairwell took them into a laundromat located directly next to the doctor's office. The place was empty and untouched by the fire that had consumed much of the town, so Rob tapped the wall to find the studs, then bashed a hole in the drywall. He peeked inside the next room.

"Looks clear."

The moment the words left his mouth, Rob quickly ducked back into the laundromat as a pair of bloody hands reached through the hole after him.

"Jesus!" Charlie sputtered and swung his assault rifle ineffectually while Smokey prepared to pull the trigger.

"Don't shoot!" Rob ordered.

The zombie, a rather average-looking guy in sweatpants, had become lodged in the hole and was now writhing like a trapped animal. Rob got to his feet, locked eyes with the creature and brought his bat down over its head with a thud. He pushed the now motionless corpse back through the hole and peeked in again, albeit more carefully this time.

"Looks clear. For real now."

The trio entered the pharmacy and Charlie searched for the supplies they needed while Rob did security. Smokey checked the zombie's body for anything useful and then joined Charlie in his search. Somehow a large stash of medicinal marijuana and various pills found their way into the duffel bag.

Soon they had what they came for and Charlie was intent on exiting in a hurry, but Smokey stopped him as they passed the body. "Dude had something on him you might want to see." Smokey pointed to some items that he'd placed on the ground.

"Cold medicine and a toy dinosaur. Who cares?"

Smokey's wheels were turning yet again. "That zombie's bite marks on his arm were fresh. He was still bleeding when Rob pounded him."

"Okay."

"So he just got turned real recently. Like within the past few minutes."

"Get to the point," Charlie said.

"Now why would someone be carrying around a toy dinosaur in their pocket?" Smokey asked.

"They like dinosaurs?" Rob answered.

"Maybe, but think about it. You're watching your kid, you're picking toys up around the house, and sometimes you put something in your pocket without thinking about it. Plus, that's kiddie cough syrup. Which means..."

"Somebody got left behind," Rob said, finishing Smokey's sentence.

"No, just no. There's a whole town in front of us and half of it is burned down. How do we even know where to begin?"

"1368 Main Street," Smokey said as he read the driver's license from the man's wallet.

"And how do you plan on finding Main Street, Columbo?"

"Look for the tallest buildings in town, there's your Main Street. Shouldn't be hard in a town this small."

Rob walked to the front of the store and looked at the signs. "Guys, we're on Main Street right now."

"We have enough problems of our own without—"

"Come on," Rob interrupted. "You know you'll give in. There's no way you'll sleep at night knowing you might have left some kid stranded like we did with Brandon."

"Stop looking at me like that. And Smokey, I can't wait for you to get stoned off your mind because this Inspector Clouseau shit is getting old fast. It's like you're an idiot savant or something when you're sober."

"Hey, we're just talking about routine investigative procedures. I have a knack for it."

Charlie was losing his patience quickly, and that often resulted in brash, horrible decisions.

Like this one.

"If I say yes, will you two stop harassing me?"

"Yep."

"Yeah."

Charlie shook his head as he went against his better judgment for the umpteenth time. "Fine, giddy up."

Chapter 7
Friends in Low Places

"Edible undies. Now there's an invention that, in theory, should have panned out a lot better than how it did in practice."

"Seriously, I can't take it anymore, Russ. Just—"

"Boy, did I have some misadventures with those things over the years," Russ interrupted Marquell, continuing on without pause as they went down yet another seemingly endless tunnel. "One pair almost killed me twice. You see, this gal and I were snacking on one of the tasty treats when I went into ana-pha, ana... I went into shock. I'm allergic to strawberries, and of course, they were lip-smacking, all-natural strawberry flavored panties. I stopped breathing and my lady friend had to call an ambulance and everything."

Trent quit shuffling along, his interest piqued. "And the second time it almost killed you?"

"The gal was my wife's sister. So, as you can imagine, the old lady had some conflicting emotions upon arriving at the hospital. That was my first wife, and she had—"

Now it was Marquell's turn to interrupt. "Shut the fuck up. You're driving me insane with this nonsense. You talk more than a prison bitch cutting hair."

"All righty then, why don't you tell us a little bit about yourself then, friend?" Russ suggested and took a quick sip of whiskey before twisting the cap back on the bottle. "We've got nothing but time down here."

"I ain't your friend. Just shut up and keep your eyes peeled. Whoever wasted my cookers might still be around." Indeed, the one surprise they had so far was coming upon the smashed glass and bullet-riddled bodies of what appeared to be Marquell's methamphetamine operation. From the looks of it, they had been dead for quite some time.

"If there is somebody down here I'll hear 'em from a ways off. Did I tell you about my superpowers since I got turned into a zombie? It's like I'm a Cherokee tracker," Russ said.

"You got the drinking part down anyways," Trent said under his breath.

Russ pointed his flashlight towards Marquell. "I heard Mr. Personality here squeak out a silent but deadly about a minute ago."

Marquell shrugged. "I guess he can hear pretty well. He's still an idiot."

Russ continued chatting about his similarities to various famous Native American heroes while Marquell bit his tongue and tried in vain to ignore him. But if the former truck driver kept it up, the violent reckoning Marquell planned would happen sooner rather than later.

They continued on, their flashlights casting long shadows down the even longer tunnel while the echoes of their footsteps bounced around the humid, musty air. The underground system was as vast as Marquell had promised, and luckily for them, the safety stations were located in regular intervals as well. This meant extra batteries, expired energy bars, and bottles of water were found every couple miles, stored away in containers directly below each handy map. Other than Russ's nonstop verbal diarrhea, the trip through the labyrinth had gone as smoothly as possible. Compared to the hell aboveground, the tomb-like tunnels were a welcome respite... even if it did smell like an old person's basement, which Trent reminded Marquell of numerous times during the hike.

Trent let Russ take the lead for once and fell back to walk by Marquell, deciding to pick the gang leader's brain a bit. "So you had some guys down here making meth? Kind of an odd location. I mean, how did you even know about this place?"

Marquell's face brightened. "Sometimes, when I got bored with the drug game, I thought about becoming an architect. I started with studying building plans and such. Then I got into making models of Frank Lloyd Wright houses with Popsicle sticks. From there I moved on to bigger venues, and that's where I got my motherfuckin' interest in civil construction projects. Anyways, I studied up on these tunnels and realized they'd be a bomb ass area for my operations. At least until they were up and running. But with government delays I knew that wouldn't be for a long time. And having a secret escape route from the city was a goal, too. Never thought I'd be down here like this, though."

Russ's flashlight flickered out and he tapped it a few times to no avail. He quickly swapped out some batteries. They didn't work, and the next batteries Russ put in failed as well. "The whole damned batch is bad. Typical government horseshit. They spend billions on these tunnels and then buy generic batteries. "

Trent's flashlight also went out, and the situation immediately turned tense as he and Russ surrounded Marquell. "All right bro, why don't you let us have the light until we find some more working batteries?"

"Hell no. End of discussion," Marquell said, his gravelly voice showing grim determination. He wasn't about to lose his newfound leverage.

Trent sighed. "Let's not turn this into a thing, okay? Don't forget that we have the guns. Now, are you picking up what I'm putting down or not?" Trent was trying his hardest to be nice, but his old d-bag self was starting to bubble up under the surface. It always did.

Marquell stood in silence as Russ got into his face. "Come on man, hand it over. It's not like we're gonna ditch you."

"I don't take orders from cops, and I definitively don't take them from hillbilly zombies dressed like motherfuckin' Captain Jack Sparrow."

"Oh hell yes, that's just what I was going for. I already had the hair, and then I found this costume after I—"

Marquell clicked his flashlight off and the tunnel was immediately as dark as the far side of the moon. So dark, in fact, that Russ didn't see Marquell's fist before it plowed into his forehead, knocking him sideways into the solid pipe wall.

It hurt Marquell's hand like crazy, but the truck driver popped back up unaffected. "Now you did it," Russ said, and prepared to shoot his Chinese assault rifle in Marquell's general direction – which also happened to be where Trent was standing.

Trent guessed what Russ was about to do and hit the musty floor. "Don't shoot, dumbass!"

Meanwhile Marquell began to tiptoe away in the darkness, trying to put some distance between himself and the others while at the same time attempting to avoid Russ's superhuman hearing. It didn't work.

"Gotcha!" Russ said as he drew a bead on the fleeing man's footsteps. But as he prepared to pull the trigger, Marquell stumbled on something and fell to the ground.

The murky abyss of the tunnel was washed away as a mysterious light streamed towards them. Next, a neon red breakdancing reindeer appeared on the wall behind the trio while a wave of sound rolled down the empty corridor. The music was loud and piercing... and it was jovial. "Feliz Navidad," to be precise.

"Laser. Fuckin. Light show," Russ said with a smile. That smile quickly disappeared as swiftly moving forms darted out from a bend in the tunnel. They were many, and they were starving.

"Drop 'em!" Trent shouted and opened up with his machine gun while Russ followed in kind. Soon out of ammo, they threw their rifles and grabbed Elvis while running towards the light, with Marquell a good distance ahead of them. The mob was slowed by the dead bodies now in their way, but undeterred all the same.

Marquell stopped ahead and the others soon caught up to him, their fight being all but forgotten. For now. He shined the remaining flashlight at the ground and revealed a gaping hole in the floor. Inside the pit were countless zombies in varying states of animation, driven mad by the festive music while squirming and jumping towards an opening that lay far from reach.

A mere fifteen-foot jump separated the men from the safety of the other side, so Marquell backed up before making the leap, and he made it look easy.

"Toss the coon over," he said.

Russ did. Then he made the jump almost as easily, with his unkempt mullet flowing behind him. Out of shape and undernourished from a diet of cat food and alcohol, Trent was unsure of his jumping abilities and wavered momentarily as the hallway behind him filled with growing shadows. He turned around and saw the horde descending towards him. It was all the encouragement Trent needed.

He took a deep breath and charged forward while letting out a mighty roar in midair. The shout was the only thing impressive about the jump, however, and he came nowhere near reaching the other side. He did manage to catch the edge of the pipe and now dangled precariously above the clawing cannibals.

Making matters worse, the zombies from behind him started tumbling into the pit at a rapid pace. As their numbers swelled, they formed a zombie ladder of sorts as those falling in stepped on each other for position, trampling the most dehydrated zombies underfoot.

Russ grabbed Trent's wrists and tried to pull him up, but he just wasn't strong enough to lift the portly officer from the deathtrap. Soon, hands tugged at Trent's boots from below and threatened to pull him to his doom.

Marquell walked toward the others and hesitated. Here was his chance to rid himself of these bumbling morons, and it would take little more than a slight shove. His mind made up, Marquell moved towards them with purpose, chuckling to himself.

Then he reached down and effortlessly dragged Trent upwards as if lifting a child from a crib. Marquell was not ready to lose his pawns quite yet.

Trent spit at the zombies and then composed himself. "Thanks, I mean it. Keep the damned flashlight."

Marquell nodded, then looked at Russ as his hand throbbed from his hard punch. "Damn, you got a hard head."

"People been telling me that my entire life."

Just then, the laser show stopped and a floodlight turned on. Several armed men crept from the pitch-black side tunnels and surrounded them. That's when a pale man wearing a bowler hat and a necklace of hickeys came to the fore with an air of superiority and malevolence. "Hands up, fuck-sticks. You're in Gutter Punk territory."

Chapter 8
Sisters

Jackie's expensive yacht powered through the choppy waters of Lake Michigan while absolute chaos erupted in the city behind them. Blaring sirens, gunfire, screams for help and explosions competed for the girls' attention before it all faded away in the distance. The whole fiasco had been going on for only about fifteen minutes.

But to Jen, Padma, Jackie, and new arrival Mary, those minutes were a lifetime. They had lost friends and dodged sudden death, and even killed a man. And it wasn't even lunchtime.

As they got some distance from the shoreline, Jen asked Jackie what they were all thinking. "Where are we going? Indiana? Michigan? Wisconsin? Just because this is your boat, it doesn't mean we don't have a say so."

Jackie cast her friend a sideways glance and continued to pilot the boat without saying a word.

"Jackie, you need to—"

"Will you let me think? Jesus," Jackie replied with a huff. She was the type that had her life in magnificent order with all going as planned since childhood, whether it was her education, career path, love life, you name it. But now that whole lifestyle was gone. There would be no more long-term plans, only reactions. Reactions based on what would keep her alive the longest. She veered left and Jen almost fell over.

"Well?"

Jackie pointed ahead at a large building rising above the water. "Here's your answer."

"Okay. What is it?"

"It's a water pumping station for the city. We'll dock here until we find out what's going on, and we can always hop back in the boat and head to shore if we need to. Does that sound good?"

"All right," Jen said and left to tell Padma what was going on.

Padma was busily tending to Mary's bruises and trying to calm the girl down. "You have a nasty knot on your head, but nothing serious," she added while checking the thirty-year-old woman's eyes. "And that's pretty amazing considering you just rode the top of a cop car and took quite a beating."

Jen grimaced upon seeing the injuries she caused the woman during their escape. "We're stopping right up here at some kind of station. It's like an artificial island. Sorry again, about that, by the way. You can't blame me though, considering."

"I'm okay," Mary said and rubbed her scalp. "It's a crazy that we ended up here together."

Jen tilted her head. "How so?"

"You don't remember me?" Mary asked, a little surprised and a little hurt.

"Sorry, no."

"I've been bagging your groceries for like ten years over at Healthy-mart. You come in like clockwork every Sunday night. Wine, cheese, waffles and soda. Anyways, I recognized you outside the store when everything started happening and figured you would know what to do. You always seem to have everything together. I chased you guys for like a mile."

"Oh yeah, Mary! It's hard to place someone when you see them out of context, you know," Jen said with half a smile. In fact, Jen didn't remember Mary at all, and couldn't care less who bagged her groceries, washed her car, or delivered her pizzas.

Mary adjusted her thick glasses and looked at the

deck, realizing the truth of the matter. It was just one more awkward snub in a lifetime of such, trivial compared to what was going on at that moment, but still painful. Friendless, basically penniless, and mentally slow, Mary was the polar opposite of her pampered companions. But now they were all in the same boat, literally.

"We're pulling up, I need some help getting tied off," Jackie shouted and the group sprang into action. Soon enough the yacht was secured in place alongside the pumping station and the women climbed onto the concrete structure, unsure of what to expect. If the growing craziness had already reached this far out, then no place was safe.

The station consisted of a large concrete loading dock with various cranes and equipment, as well as an ornately built, circular stone building. Water was collected inside and transported by tunnel to a filtration plant, hundreds of feet beneath Lake Michigan. A small bridge led to a smaller, now defunct pumping station. But the women weren't interested in the functions and purpose of the place. For now, they were more concerned with discovering if it was safe.

They were about to find out. The door to the building shot open and a man and a woman wearing hardhats came towards them.

"You can't dock here! This is a restricted area. Did you not see the damned signs?" the man asked. "You can get jail time just for being here. Homeland Security will have your—"

"Nobody's going to jail, Frank," a woman named Carol said in a much less combative tone. "You do need to leave, though. This center is off limits."

Jackie shook her head. "We're not going anywhere. Don't you know what's going on in the city? It's like a warzone right now. People are acting nuts, it's out of control."

"See, this girl's on drugs," Frank said and threw his

hands up. "Just because you have a fancy boat doesn't mean the rules don't apply to you. I suppose you're related to somebody important too?"

"Actually, my dad is Jessie Collins. He used to be the congre—"

"I know who he is and I don't care. Now I'm not gonna listen to your tall tales anymore. We're supposed to be running the station, not talking to drunken socialites on a joy ride."

"Guys," Mary said quietly. She was ignored in the scrum, as she had been countless times in her everyday life.

Frank's co-worker stepped in again. "Let's just take things down a notch and get this sorted out. I can make some phone calls."

"Guys!" Mary screamed at the top of her lungs and pointed. Everyone on the platform turned to see a low-flying airliner heading in their direction, rapidly losing altitude. The noise was deafening as it banked sharply and crashed into the water directly in front of the station.

The plane violently broke into pieces as debris and water splashed upwards and then came down like hail. One of the still roaring engines broke free and skipped across the water before bouncing up and over the group of terrified onlookers. That is, mostly over. Carol and Frank were gone, and all that remained were their shoes. And their feet.

"Holy shit," Jen said as Mary gagged before puking forcefully.

That's when they noticed the survivors of the crash. Several had floated to the surface, severely injured and screaming.

"We should try to save them!" Padma said, her doctor's instincts kicking in. She started taking her clothes off in order to dive into the churning mess, but one by one the screaming victims ceased their struggling and disappeared under the water.

About a minute later several began to reemerge, and then a few more. Soon dozens of passengers calmly bobbed up and down in the surf and debris as the smell of jet-fuel became overpowering. Padma walked to the edge of the dock and prepared to jump in.

Jackie grabbed her shoulder. "Wait, something's not right. They're quiet now."

"Fine." Padma waved her arms over her head instead. "Swim over here!" The survivors started to dog paddle towards the pumping station as they heard her voice. "You okay?" she asked.

There was no answer and Jackie shook her head, a grim look on her face. "See?"

"Say something, anything!" Padma yelled, but there was still no reply from any of the injured people. No screams, no pained whimpers, nothing. Just quiet swimming and expressionless faces. Now they were within ten yards of the ladder, close enough that the girls could see their injuries, including multiple bite marks.

Jackie immediately pointed her flare gun at the growing jet-fuel slick and fired, setting the swimmers ablaze in an instant. The zombies didn't have the sense to dive away from the flames and burned up in the inferno. Unfortunately the current brought the flames right up to Jackie's yacht, and in seconds it too was engulfed.

The yacht smoldered for a while as the women sat and watched, stunned by their sudden loss. Then Jackie's boat, called *Obsidian* for her favorite color, slipped into Lake Michigan and disappeared from sight. With it went all hope of escape.

*   *   *

Mary flicked her wrist and pushed the knife in effortlessly as the warm guts spilled onto the dock. The three-pound rainbow trout shuttered briefly and went still. It wasn't much for four adults, but it was dinner.

A week had passed since they'd been stranded on the pumping station. The girls had little clue of what was transpiring in the rest of the world, and it was probably a good thing. The United States had been overrun by a manmade virus and simultaneously invaded by China, it had nuked its enemies in retaliation, and Charlie and his friends had settled into a life of cat food and expired beer.

But getting marooned at the pumping station had been more than a little lucky. Mary and the others had found themselves isolated from the rampaging hordes of cannibals and separated from the fires and looting in the city. In addition, the place was equipped with canned goods, drinking water, and two comfortable bedrooms. The late Frank had even left behind his fishing rod and lures, which Mary was using to great effect in order to supplement their meals of corn and baked beans.

It was a tedious existence, but it was safe – for the time being, anyway. If the lake froze during the winter, however, things would rapidly take a turn for the worse. And so ideas for escape were never far from their thoughts.

For now, though, dinner took precedence and Mary brought the catch of the day in to be cooked on a propane grill. Her fishing skills had come in handy and earned her respect from Jackie and Padma... but not so much from Jen.

Over the past few years Jen had grown more like her stuck up fiancé, Blake, and Mary proved to be an easy target for her diatribes. She had a snide comment for everything the newcomer did, whether it was how she dressed, talked, cooked, or even slept. Right now it was the way Mary was singing hymns while cooking fish.

"You never shut up, do you? I'm surprised you don't get sun burns on your tongue."

"Jen, come on," Padma chided as Mary looked down and mumbled something under her breath.

"I just don't see what's worth singing about at the moment. This sucks. I'm bored out of my mind, it's hot as hell, who knows if we'll ever get off this dump, and god knows what will happen if we do."

Padma touched her friend's shoulder. "We all deal with grief in different ways."

"I can sing if I want to," Mary chimed in.

"Shhh, the grownups are talking," Jen shot back.

"I'm a grown—"

"Grownups don't push shopping carts into corrals, sweetie."

Padma's attractive face hardened. "Why don't you wake Jackie and tell her it's almost time to eat?"

Jen rolled her eyes and left as Padma started singing with Mary and took over grilling the fish. A few minutes later everyone gathered on the dock for their meager dinner as the sun sank over the horizon. Far away, skyscrapers burned brightly as the artificial clouds of destruction billowed across the heavens. It would almost be pretty if one could ignore the macabre implications.

Jackie yawned loudly and asked if anything exciting had happened while she rested for her graveyard watch. It hadn't. And so they fell into their nightly ritual of eating bland food while "enjoying" even blander conversation.

"I miss my cat," Mary said as she picked at the corn on her plate, bringing up yet another topic nobody else gave a damn about. "I hope she was able to escape my apartment. Maybe through the window or something."

"What was her name?" Jackie asked as Jen made rude faces.

Mary brightened, happy that at least someone was paying attention to her. This was something that had rarely happened even before the apocalypse. "I called her

Little Mama. I got her a few months ago when a neighbor was getting rid of her for peeing on the carpet."

"And you thought it was a good idea to take in a cat that was gonna... oh I guess I'm wasting my breath," Jen said.

Mary shook her head. "You shouldn't throw away things just because they're not perfect. Nobody's perfect. Not even you."

"Please, screw your pity party," Jen said as her voice rose. "If anyone should be depressed, it's me. I lost a fantastic life and a handsome man. What did you lose? A cat-piss apartment and a dead-end job? Heck, you might be better off now."

Mary had heard enough and decided to stick up for herself for once. "Girls like you have picked on me my entire life, and why? Because I'm not smart or pretty like you? Because I had to wear the same clothes to school every day? Well, you're stuck with me now so you're going to have to just learn to deal with it."

"You weren't exactly invited along."

"Why are you, you, you... being so nasty?" Mary said and began to turtle up as the all-too-familiar feelings of suffocation crept in. It was times like this when her stuttering made an unwelcome appearance.

"Because you're annoy—"

"Shut your damned mouth and lay off her," Jackie said, having grown tired of Jen's bullying. "We've been friends for years, pledge sisters, and you wanted me in your wedding. But I'm telling you, shut it now or I will shut it for you. Blake's friends might enjoy treating each other like shit all the time, but that's not how I'm going to live my life. We're better than that."

"She's right, we simply must get along if we want to survive, all of us," Padma added.

Jen's shoulders sank and she let out a deep sigh. "Padma was right. We all cope with grief differently, and I think maybe my way is being a cunty bitch. My bad."

"Hug it out," Jackie said. The two women did, albeit reluctantly, and the tension dropped immediately.

"Girls' night!" Jen said and laughed awkwardly. "We don't have liquor, so let's do makeup."

"We don't have makeup either," Jackie said.

"The lady that got cut in half over there had a bunch in her locker," Jen said. "I kind of hid it from you all. Sorry."

Mary was tentative. "I've never worn makeup before."

"O-M-G. Then you get to go first," Jen said and smiled at her with genuine warmth. "I have a great idea on what we can do with you. Nothing bold, but I think you'll like it all the same."

Minutes later they were applying and primping and laughing, with Mary being the loudest of them all. No, she didn't look very pretty – she was still as plain as vanilla and pigeon-toed like no other – but she sure felt marvelous. And there was something to be said for that.

Caught up in the moment, nobody noticed the small boat arriving on the far side of the station. Two men tied off and moved in the direction of the laughter and lanterns.

Chapter 9
Three Morons and a Baby

The idea to look for the abandoned child was settled, but the method of doing so had not been. After some arguing and mild swearing, Smokey convinced his friends he would hotwire the lone car in the parking lot. "Time me," he said and ran outside. The car door was unlocked and Smokey slid into the driver's seat. Less than thirty seconds later the brake lights came on and Cher could be heard blasting on the stereo before he could shut the CD player off.

"Ugh, she's the worst," Charlie said as he and Rob climbed into the red Dodge Caliber. "And before you even say something stupid I realize you probably learned that from watching some dumbass show. So let's just get on with it," he added. "And good job, that was fast. You being a worthless turd the past ten years has saved our lives I don't know how many times now."

"I was yanking your chain. Found the keys in the dead dude's pocket," Smokey said while smiling deeply and pulling away. He hadn't gotten much validation in his life, and it was a nice feeling. Even if he had been called a turd.

"Well, good job anyways, now let's find the place." Charlie grabbed Smokey's rifle and scanned the streets of Biggsburg for any movement, cannibal or otherwise. The place seemed to be a ghost town though, and they travelled a few blocks without so much as a squirrel crossing their path.

"Man, if we could just get to the interstate and haul

ass, we could be at my parents' house in an hour," Charlie said, thinking out loud.

"But the roads aren't safe," Rob countered. "And Left-Nut needs us. And Sam. And maybe a kid."

"I know, I know. It would just be nice. That's all I'm saying. Get to my mom and dad's and the military base is right past it."

"Soon," Rob said, showing a bit of wisdom that usually eluded him like so many cheeseburgers had not. "You'll see her soon. She has to be safer at that base than anywhere else right now."

Smokey pulled up to an intersection and, sure enough, Main Street was the road with the taller buildings on it. Now they just had to look for the address, which according to the numbers was just a block or so away.

"Can't get any easier than this."

"Don't jinx it," Rob said.

Seconds later they stopped in front of an apartment building and got out. Smokey checked the mailbox to determine the right apartment and the others followed him through the shattered front door and up a set of stairs. Other than the door, nothing seemed out of place except the complete silence. They soon found apartment 2A right by the stairs.

Smokey jiggled the handle and it was locked, so he pulled up the welcome mat featuring a tropical beach and produced a key as Charlie rolled his eyes. He slowly pushed the door open and backed up while Rob stepped forward, ready to bash any surprises this time. But there was only dead silence.

The guys walked inside. "Hello?" Charlie said quietly, but there was no answer. The place looked as though it had been recently lived in, and there was a bag of garbage by the front door that had no rotting food in it. There were toys scattered around, but no kid.

Smokey checked the garbage bag and pulled out several boxes. "Grape cough syrup," he said. "Trent and I used

76

to drink that stuff and get high as rainclouds. That's Robo-tripping for you nerds. Anyways, one night he thought there were clowns behind him in the mirror, and that was the last time we did that."

"Very interesting," Charlie said dryly and shrugged. "But this place is empty. Look for anything useful and let's jet." He looked to Rob. "At least we checked."

Smokey wasn't so sure. "Hold up, partner." He pointed to a family picture on the mantel. There was the man Rob had killed in the doctor's office, standing with a woman and a small child. Another frame showed off a picture of a chubby baby boy with the name Todd written on it.

"Toddy, where are you, buddy? I got some candy," Smokey said in a funny voice. Faint giggling could be heard coming from the living room closet. He opened the door and found the one-year-old snuggled up in dinosaur blankets.

"We found him, now what?" Charlie said. "Maybe his mom is out somewhere, like the dad. She comes home and the baby's gone and her husband's dead. Talk about a tearjerker. Plus, then we're baby stealers."

"Nah, normal parents wouldn't both leave their child behind like that," Smokey said. He tried to pick the kid up, and it became immediately clear what the cough syrup had been used for. Little Todd became startled by the unknown man and erupted in a level of sound and fury that was quite substantial for a tot that size.

"Shut that kid up," Charlie said as flashbacks of the Brandon incident came blasting into his mind. Noise equaled zombies equaled death.

"Like, how?" Smokey asked. He wasn't the type of person a sober parent would let watch their kid, and so his time with young ones was extremely limited.

"Give him something to play with," Charlie said and looked for a suitable toy on the floor.

Smokey handed Mr. Personality the car keys to shake, but the kid was not amused, and screamed even louder – if that was possible.

"Dude was giving the kid medicine to keep it quiet, like that chick in Florida," Rob surmised. "That's messed up."

Charlie looked out the window and shook his head. "True, but I wish we had some." Like he'd expected, the tantrum had zombies already gathering outside, and many began finding their way through the broken front door. In no time the hungry beasts would pinpoint their location.

"Oh, duh," Smokey said and produced a small dinosaur toy from his pocket. It was a plush T-rex, and the one Todd's father had in his pocket upon reaching his final destination. The baby grabbed the toy and calmed down as shambling footsteps came up the stairs and stopped outside their door. Everyone held their breath until the cannibals could be heard walking back down the stairs.

And then little Toddy squeaked the toy, loudly and repeatedly. The zombies came back with a vengeance, pounding on the flimsy door and threatening to burst in at any second.

"Shit, shit, shit!" Charlie looked outside to see several zombies milling about below the window, cutting off their route back to the car. "Shit! I knew this was a dumb idea."

"What's the plan?" Smokey asked.

"Kick ass, take names," Rob said casually. He wasn't much of a planner, but he was an ass kicker.

Charlie nodded. "Okay, but... what the hell?"

Rob jumped out the second story window and obliterated a zombie with his bat on the way down. Two quick swings left two more dead cannibals that didn't even know what hit them. But a fourth one got in close, much too close, and Rob was forced to grab the lady by the throat. He squeezed and squeezed until his hand sunk through the woman's skin and into her flesh. Rob felt the prickly vertebrae and whipped his wrist to the side, breaking the teacher aide's neck in twain. He dropped the tiny woman and rubbed his hands on the grass, then massaged his throbbing and badly sprained ankle.

Now Rob was outside and alone, and the others were inside and still trapped. He waved up and whispered, "Jump down, I'll catch you."

"Why not?" Charlie gripped his rifle tightly in his hands and took a leap of faith. Rob caught him easily but put even more strain on his ankle in the process.

Now it was Smokey's turn, and of course, he was absolutely terrified of heights. So he hesitated in the window while gently rocking the baby, and tried to muster up the courage to jump.

Charlie glared at Rob. "You just crossed that thin line between bravery and stupidity. Acting like the hero is gonna get you killed. So knock it off, this ain't a movie."

"Like when Russ saved everyone? Or when you rescued Brandon?" Rob said while swiveling around, searching for any more threats.

Charlie nodded. "Yeah, I'm guilty too. Look, there's a time for reacting and a time for planning things out. Just try to follow my lead. That being said, holy crap, that was awesome."

Rob set the kill-stick down and opened his arms wide. "Smokey, if you don't jump I'm gonna punch you silly the next time I see you. Remember what I did to Trent?"

As he talked, a heavily smashed but not thoroughly dead zombie crawled up behind him. The mess of a taxi driver moved slowly enough to go unnoticed, and would soon be within striking distance. Although its eyes had been knocked clear out if its head by Rob's bat, it could evidently still hear and smell him quite clearly. And to a zombie, Rob was a whole mountain of meat, a veritable smorgasbord.

Rob's pep talk was enough and Smokey ultimately jumped, clutching on to the toddler for dear life while wearing a backpack full of diapers and toys.

"Did somebody order a manny?" he said upon landing, happy to be on the ground for sure.

Suddenly the nightmarish zombie lunged forward as Rob was distracted, but he didn't get far.

"Sorry buddy, not today," Charlie said and curb-stomped the pitiful thing into oblivion, splattering it onto the pavement like a June bug.

Things were looking up until little Toddy started screaming again as the shock from the fall wore off and his stranger danger kicked back in. This kid had some serious lungs on him too.

"Let's ride," Charlie said urgently as several zombies made their way from the building. Smokey looked at Todd and his eyes got big.

"Where's the keys?" Charlie asked.

"Um, the baby had them. I guess they're still in the apartment.

"Now *that's* the Smokey I remember," Charlie said. Three runners approached and he was forced to use up the last of the QBZ-95 ammunition. Two fell instantly, but one kept coming despite massive internal bleeding. So Charlie pulled his newly acquired pistol from his pocket and grinned, Indiana Jones like.

It promptly misfired due to the burr on the inside of the magazine that caused a feeding issue. Charlie didn't know that –he simply knew the bullet didn't come out. He palmed the useless hunk of metal and bashed the creature's face in, kicking it once for the hell of it. "There's too many, we'll have to hoof it," he added, unaware of Rob's injury.

With no other options, the slightly overweight substitute teacher, the three-hundred-pound plus pound MMA fighter with an injured ankle, and the pot smoking know-it-all carrying a baby took off at a rather dismal speed.

"We need to make it about a mile and then we can lose them in the forest," Charlie said while slowing down for his friends. At that point he noticed Rob's limp, and knew then and there that they wouldn't make it.

The lead zombie was gaining on them, so Charlie doubled back and hammered it with his empty rifle, using the thing's own speed against it but falling down in the process. He got up and caught the others as they passed the strip mall parking lot and entered the field behind it. Todd had been screaming the entire way, and more zombies joined the chase.

The tree line was just a quarter of a mile off, but Rob wasn't going to make it. His lungs burned, his ankle was even worse off than it had been, and he was close to having a heart attack. Not to mention he was hungry.

Rob stopped running. "You guys go."

"No way, Charlie said. "Maybe I can get them chasing me in another direction."

"Not with the kid screaming. No, you go," Rob said with determination and sadness etched on his face.

"I'm not—"

"Now!" The matter clearly wasn't up for discussion, but Charlie had already lost too many friends, and so he lingered.

"Go!" Rob shoved hard against his best friend's chest as Smokey disappeared into the forest and the zombies got closer.

Charlie nodded. "Fine. I told you this hero shit would get you killed." Tears ran freely down his face. "Fucking Left-Nut."

"Later, muchacho." His features hardening, the Titan of the Midwest, Viking Rob Magnusson, went into beast mode one final time as Charlie ran off, unable to look back.

All alone, Rob spit on his hands and lifted his trusty bat, bent and dinged from countless kill shots. The mob closed in, but the giant didn't wait for them. Instead, he roared an improvised battle cry and charged, ignoring the pain in his ankle and the natural instinct to flee. This man truly had been born in the wrong era.

The battle was met and Rob smashed two skulls with the first swing, and the force whipped him around in a full circle whereupon he obliterated a third with the same glorious blow. Next he brought the bat up and down as if chopping wood, dropping foes one bloody explosion at a time.

They kept coming, Rob kept swinging and the bodies piled up like dirty dishes. But the adrenaline soon ebbed and he began to grow tired. His swings slowed and some of the infected got up again, having been stunned, not killed. He pounded them again, even stomped a few for good measure. But they kept coming. The crimson bat slipped from Rob's tired grasp as he fell to his knees, and they kept coming.

One nightmarish beast lurched from Rob's side and he didn't even see it. But Charlie did, and he hammered it with the butt end of his machine gun, finishing it off with a couple of clumsy bashes.

"Never leave a man behind, remember?" he said while helping his friend rise.

"Acting like a hero's gonna get you killed, Chuck," Rob said and beamed a smile, partially reinvigorated.

"No shit," Charlie answered as the final half-dozen stragglers attacked all at once.

The problem was that Charlie was built for speed, not fighting, and as the melee got hot and heavy he was getting in the way more than helping. At one point, he barely avoided getting himself maimed by stepping into Rob's kill zone, and ended up dropping his awkwardly shaped assault rifle at the worst possible moment. Forced to grapple with a biter, he was lucky that it was smaller and weaker. Even so, Charlie ended up on his back with the slobbering fiend searching for an opening.

Machinegun fire erupted and bullets whizzed around the combatants. It wasn't clear who the targets were, but

Charlie felt his opponent go limp and warm blood gush down onto his own face. He wondered if the next bullet had his name on it.

Then there was some hurried shouting in a coarse, foreign language. Charlie pushed the body aside and stood up next to Rob as Chinese soldiers emerged from the forest, their weapons raised.

"Fuckbucket," Rob said.

They were captured, and in deep shit, but at least they were alive. For now.

Chapter 10
Fine Dining

Trent instantly knew who the scoundrel was before him. It was not a good thing. Even worse, the leader of the Gutter Punks recognized him in turn.

"Well, lick my gnads and call me Choppy. If it isn't the biggest asshole cop in all of Chicago. My old buddy, Officer Trent. Or as I once called him, Officer Gank, for ganking my dope every chance he got."

"Hello, Xavier," Trent said in a subdued tone. "Nice place you have down here."

"This isn't a dialogue," Xavier said and turned to his men. "Tie 'em up. If anyone gives you problems, throw their ass in the pit." His henchmen quickly pilfered everything of value from the trio and led them to an opening in the pipe, which happened to be an access station to the surface. Littered with crappy furniture, horror movie posters, and empty bottles, it resembled an unkempt teenager's basement bedroom. But the reality was much, much darker.

The Gutter Punks were an informal gang that had made the Clockwork Orange crew look like amateurs even before the apocalypse. Afterwards, their depravities had grown tenfold. This group of maladjusted hooligans used to ride the trains into the city every spring from out west, looking to drink, fight, forage, and fuck their way to notoriety, and not necessarily in that order. Now the man-bun-wearing hipster douches were the lords of the underground, raiding Chicago from below while keeping one-step ahead of the zombies and foreign invaders.

Trent and company were handcuffed to a steel pipe as the Gutter Punks hurled insults, garbage, and several solid punches. Xavier grabbed the raccoon and began gently stroking her head. "So well mannered. I hope it tastes good too."

"Elvis, sic balls!" Russ shouted in desperation, but the raccoon merely licked Xavier's face. "Damn."

Xavier nodded to one of the lower ranking members of the group, a fat teenager wearing face paint. "Jester, we're gonna show our little friend here the kitchen. Let me know if they have anything interesting to share. If they don't, I'll be back in a bit to ask some questions myself. With a blowtorch." He rubbed Trent's hair and left, taking the other members of the gang with him.

This left Trent, Marquell and Russ in the dimly lit room with the guy known affectionately as Jester. The giggling teen with a ninth-grade education was happy to have a captive audience for once, and was bound and determined not to screw up.

Trent had always told people he hated clowns, when in reality they scared him half to death. This meant Jester's clown makeup was terrorizing the crap out of him.

The young thug noticed that Trent's eyes were plastered shut. "What's wrong, piggy?"

Trent kept his mouth closed as well, which of course was something Russ was physically incapable of doing.

"What's with the face paint?" Russ asked. "You part of the KISS Army or something?"

Jester rolled his eyes. "KISS? What decade do you think this is?"

"That's what I said," Marquell noted to nobody in particular.

"If you really want to know, I'm a Juggalo. Maybe the last one," Jester answered with pride.

Marquell whispered something and the pride in the teen's voice turned to a threat of violence. "Got something to say, smart mouth?"

"Just the Lord's prayer." To Marquell's trained ear, it was obvious the young man was a weakling and a follower, one that was only playing the ruffian while using his false bravado to hide the scared child underneath. And so Marquell kept the discourse open, something that had saved his own life numerous times. "Why do they call you Jester? he continued.

The Gutter Punk smiled, happy to be talking about his favorite subject. "It's 'cause I like to tell jokes. Before the end of the world I wanted to be a comedian or an actor."

"I got some good ones for you," Russ said. "Who was the country singer with the biggest boobs? Conway Titty."

Jester groaned. "Weak."

"Okay, that was kind of a dad joke I guess," Russ said. "You'll like this one, though. What do you call a thousand lesbians with machine guns?"

"I'll bite. What?" Jester asked, trying to hold back a grin.

"Militia Etheridge," Russ said, already laughing at his own joke. It became so quiet you could hear the zombies scratching at the walls in the pit. "Hey, comedy's hard, you got anything better?"

Jester broke into a reasonably good Andrew Dice Clay impersonation. "You know, date rape drugs aren't all they're cracked up to be. When I take 'em I can't even stand up, let alone rape anyone. Oh!"

Russ and Marquell fake laughed at Jester's performance while Trent still cowered in fear. After a few minutes sharing more of his terrible jokes, the comedian wannabe let his guard down ever so slightly. "Look, I'm not that bad of a person, but these guys were the last people around. It was either fit in or die."

Now Trent began to wonder if the kid was playing "good cop/bad cop" with them, a tactic he had done countless times himself. He decided to find out, and slowly opened his eyes. "Hey, buddy. Why don't you let us go? You can come with us and get a fresh start. Nobody can live in a tunnel forever. Except for rats. You don't look like a rat to me."

"Sorry, dude. I can't risk it. But let me know some good info and I can probably make things easier for you. I mean, you guys aren't so bad. I feel sorry for what they're gonna do to you."

"What's that?" Trent asked.

"You're probably better off not knowing, but that raccoon is gonna be the appetizer. We don't exactly get a lot of fresh protein down here."

"For real? I survived zombies and now I'm gonna get eaten by scurveball dipshits?"

"Gutter Punks and cops just never got along. Like a cats and dogs type of thing. Plus, it sounds like Xavier hates you with a passion."

"What about me? I ain't no pig," Marquell said.

"How do I put this? You didn't pass the blackground check."

Marquell shook his head. "Is everybody in this damned tunnel racist?"

"Hey, I'm not racist," Russ said. "My second wife was black. Hell, one of my kids was black. At least I think he was my kid. He was pretty damned tall come to think of it. Either way, I had to pay child support. I mean, I was supposed to pay child support."

"Shut it, hillbilly," Jester said, switching back to bully-mode once more. He realized time was running short and his task was still unfulfilled, which meant Xavier was just as likely to use the blowtorch on him. He was a dick like that.

"Thank you," Marquell added.

Jester got into Marquell's face. "As I said, I'm looking for useful stuff. Like, if you have a stash outside or a safe house or something. And what Xavier wants most are females. They don't last very long down here on account of—"

Russ cut him off. "They already took my stash. Two-fifths of whiskey, one flask of rum. Mostly cheap stuff, but it sure gets the job done. Hell, I bet they're getting drunk as skunks right now."

"And they didn't want to share it with you," Marquell said, stirring the pot. "Not very nice of them. I guess you're the low man on the totem pole."

"For reals? Man, you're full of it."

"Honest," Marquell said and pointed to Russ. "You can smell that Joe Dirt looking motherfucker's breath. He was drinking all damned day."

Alcohol was the one thing that kept Jester going, so he turned to Russ and leaned in, breathing deeply. "He does smell like a hobo that just... argh!"

Russ's head shot forward and he chomped down hard, ripping away Jester's painted nose as well as his upper lip. It was obvious the truck driver savored every bite as his eyes rolled into the back of his head.

The young man slumped to his knees in shock and convulsed, instinctively pulling the trigger on his pistol. The bullet blew a hole in Jester's foot and he fell the rest of the way down, landing on his ruined face. He had told his last joke.

Russ's feral hunger sated, he snapped back into the moment, licking his lips. "Juggalo? More like Juggalicious. We're talking Arby's Big Montana right there. Could've used some Horsey Sauce though."

"Okay, now what, smart guys?" Trent asked as Jester writhed around, moaning for his momma.

"Ask Marquell, this is his plan. He told me to bite the dude," Russ said.

Just then a Gutter Punk brandishing a machete burst through the door at the sound of gunfire. "What's wrong with Jester?" he asked.

"Case of the Mondays?" Marquell suggested, buying some time.

Trent shrugged. "Nah, looks like it's a Shaq attack."

"Real funny." The man saw the massive amount of blood and advanced towards Trent, raising his blade to strike. "Let's see who's laughing when I cut your tongue out."

Jester rose and jumped onto the young man's back, ripping into his neck and feeding on the soft tissues underneath. Moments later more Gutter Punks ran in, but they were met by Jester and his victim, now a zombie as well. It was a bloodbath, and when Trent saw Jester's mangled clown-face going to work he had to shut his eyes once more to avoid passing out from fear.

Soon the feeding frenzy would grow and the tied up men would be dropping to the bottom of the food chain. Realizing this, Russ did something drastic. He leaned over and started chewing on the bottom half of his own left hand, grinding through bones and tearing through flesh. Unflinching, he yanked hard on his hand, and what remained of it slid through the handcuff while his pinky and ring finger dropped the ground. Russ's third wedding ring rolled across the tunnel floor and made the tiniest of clinks as it bounced off the wall, never to be seen again.

Xavier and the rest of his men came in and were immediately set upon. But they were better prepared and put up a fight, blasting away at the cannibals that had been their allies minutes before.

Trent and Marquell yanked on their own handcuffs as the carnage in the small room daisy chained. Jester stopped chewing on his latest victim and made a beeline for Marquell, who was forced to jump into the air and kick with both feet. The freak show plowed into Xavier, who then shoved him towards Trent.

Jester grabbed Trent and bit down, but his face exploded outwards in a shower of wet mush. Russ had shot the zombie with its own pistol. Then he turned and fired three shots, dropping two zombies and one Gutter Punk.

The door to the tunnel creaked open and Russ turned to see Xavier sprinting away with the last of the zombies chasing after him, drawn by his rapid movements. Russ shut the door and surveyed the massacre. The whole battle had taken less than a minute.

"Seriously Marquell, that was like some *Tango and Cash* shit right there," he said and beamed a reddish smile. "Mumbling the plan, knowing that only I could catch it with my badass hearing."

"Man, I don't even know what that means. Just find the handcuff keys."

Russ searched the corpses, found the keys, and released his companions. Then he took a filthy shirt from one of the bodies and made a tourniquet for his hand while the others gathered weapons and ammo. Though he didn't feel the pain, Russ could still pass out from the loss of blood, and so getting the wound closed up was important.

"Looks like we're done down here," Trent said and got no arguments. "Let's find Elvis and roll out." They opened the door to the lair of the Gutter Punks and noticed it was even more of a pigsty than the last room. Small lamps lit the area, as did a working gas grill, and the scent of cooked meat was thick in the confined space. It actually smelled pretty good.

"Awww, those bastards." Russ slumped to the floor when he spotted the freshly slaughtered animal carcass on the rack. Grilled to perfection and seasoned with salt and pepper.

Trent put a hand to his friend's shoulder as it became apparent that, yes, zombies can cry. The cop even felt an odd flood of emotion for an animal he cared little for, though his mouth watered at the smell of the meal.

"What are y'all busters crying about?" Marquell asked as he poked around for supplies, finding little of use.

"Elvis... has left the building," Russ said with a shudder.

Marquell nodded and gave them a moment to grieve. Then he pulled the meat off the fire, blew on it forcefully,

90

and took a bite. Maybe it was a little payback for what had happened to his friend.

"Oh, no you didn't," Russ said and rose to his feet, his good hand clenched in a fist. "That ain't kosher."

Marquell casually pointed to the corner of the room. There, next to a dirty sleeping bag, a raccoon was happily licking up a spilled bottle of maple syrup.

Russ grinned creepily and wiped the tears from his face with his bandaged stump, leaving behind a glob of coagulated blood.

"Not to change the subject, but Trent, when you find yourself hundreds of feet underground during a zombie apocalypse and you're still running into people that hate you, it might be time for a life change. And that's coming from me."

"I'm trying, Russ. I'm trying," Trent said and took a bite of the roasted tunnel rat. It was a bit salty and a bit gamey, but damn was it delicious.

"Eating rats in the actual sewer. Winning."

He and Marquell ate the carcass in under a minute and then pilfered what meager supplies they could while Russ retrieved his liquor.

The trio and their trusty mascot opened the exit door and then climbed the spiral stairs for quite a while until they reached the top. Eventually they exited the access building and walked outside into the cool night air, finding themselves mere miles from the suburbs. They had done the near impossible, but in some ways their journey had only just begun.

Russ pointed dead ahead and grinned. "That might be the prettiest damned thing I've ever seen."

Chapter 11
Strange Nerds with Candy

"Permission to come aboard?" someone said from the dark as two flashlights illuminated the startled women. Of course, the intruders were already standing in the middle of the water pumping station, so the question was moot.

"Dammit," Jackie swore as she stood up quickly and grabbed her crowbar, assuming a defensive stance. She had insisted on keeping a vigilant watch, and now their security had been blown by a moment of carelessness.

"Relax there," one of the men said reassuringly. "I'm Phil, this is Bobby, and we're here to rescue you... if you need rescuing. that is." Both middle-aged men had awkward demeanors and were dressed like they just got off the golf course. "Does anyone have a sweet tooth?" he continued and tossed a handful of snack-sized candy bars to the women.

They tore into the treats and breathed a collective, yet guarded, sigh of relief. Someone had finally come to get them, even if they were dorky. Still, the women had some questions for the strangers bearing gifts.

"What's going on out there?" Padma asked. "Last Sunday we were minding our own business and then things just went berserk. Is the government getting things under control?"

Phil casually approached and sat down on an upturned five gallon bucket. He looked like a younger version of Weird Al Yankovic. "We don't actually know. It seems that no place on land is safe. And we haven't seen anyone from the government other than some dead sheriff's deputies at one of the harbors. We're on our own for now, which is why we're out looking for survivors. Trying to pitch in."

"It's like something from a horror movie," Bobby added. He was still hanging back a little and fidgeting with his watch. "Kids eating their parents, neighbors killing each other over bread, no electricity..."

"Then how can you rescue us?" Padma asked. "We are entirely isolated out here. We should probably just stay put."

Phil nodded. "True, it is isolated, but how much food do you have?" Nobody answered and he continued, "We've got a pretty big houseboat and lots of supplies. Bobby's wife and kids and my girlfriend are there as we speak. You'd have to pull your own weight, but if it's just the four of you, we have enough room."

"Yeah, it's just us," Mary said without thinking.

Jackie cringed inside. "She means it's just us inside right now. My boyfriend and a few others are out hunting for supplies and should be back any minute. We'll tell them about your offer, though."

"Is that so?" Phil said and smiled, revealing a set of horribly crooked teeth that clashed with his outwardly preppy appearance. "I guess we better get on with it then." He stood up and produced a pistol tucked underneath his shirt. "You see, those things about the houseboat and the wife and kids are true. But the part about you coming with us, well that part's bullshit." He took a step back and cocked his gun.

Bobby did the same and it became obvious they were more pirate than nerd. "Toss that crowbar in the lake. Anyone else that has a weapon should do the same. If I find anything dangerous on you in a minute, it's gonna be used against you."

Mary tossed her knife into the drink and Bobby proceeded to check the women, lingering whenever and

93

however he wanted during the search. His breath smelled like an odd combination of whiskey and stinky cheese, and his body odor was even worse.

Phil seemed rather pleased with himself for having taken total control of the situation. "So now we're gonna be grabbing whatever food you have and we'll be on our way. We have mouths to feed, after all." He pointed to Jackie. "Take Bobby with you to where you store it. If you're not back in two minutes then one of your friends will be wishing you had been."

Jackie nodded and took the man to the station's pantry where she handed over three cans of baked beans. They walked back to the others and Bobby set the goods down one at a time on a bench.

Phil took a look at the cans and fired his pistol at Jackie's head, missing her by inches. "You think I'm some kind of idiot? I'm supposed to believe with four grown women out here all you've got to eat is three cans of beans?"

"That's it, you can search the whole place if you'd like, but we have no other food," Jackie said, contemplating a wild charge at the man. She believed she could take him with a little luck, and maybe even wrestle the gun away while her friends tackled Bobby.

But there was no time for heroics as Phil pointed his pistol at Padma. "I'm gonna count to three, and if someone doesn't tell me where the rest of the food is, I'm gonna blow her damned brains out. One. Two. Thr—"

"Fine, I'll take you to the food," Jackie said. "Will you leave us then?"

"We'll leave when we get what we came for."

Jackie took Phil across the bridge to the outdated and abandoned second pumping station. Inside the old building was a large hole that had previously been the water intake section. Jackie grabbed a rope that dangled into the lake and pulled a fishing net out. It was crammed with canned goods of all types.

"Jackpot," Phil said. "My wife's gonna give me a big hug when I show up with this stuff." He took the bounty back to the others while holding Jackie at gunpoint.

"Nice grab," Bobby said and gave him a fist bump.

Jackie pressed her luck. "That's it. Now you have everything you came for."

Phil looked into her furious brown eyes. "No... not everything."

"What's are you getting at?"

"There's just a little matter of your punishment for not telling the truth," Phil said as his geeky face hardened.

The lust in Bobby's eyes was undeniable. "I always wanted a harem. Nice little selection here too. Very exotic."

These men had been invisible their entire lives, and now they had a chance to correct all their old grievances, real and imagined, against the finer sex. "Sweetheart, the next time a man with a gun asks you for something, give it to him," Phil said to Jackie. Then he looked at each girl for an uncomfortable moment before settling on Mary. "You. You're not as pretty as the others, but at least you have some damned makeup on."

"All tarted up for a night out on the town," Bobby added with a snicker.

"Would have been nice if you other tramps put forth some effort. Maybe next time. Grab her and let's go," Phil said and pointed to their boat, a small charter fishing vessel they had commandeered during the outbreak.

Jen had remained quiet the entire time, but chose this moment to step forward. The reason was simple: she knew Mary was a virgin. So, feeling guilty about her own actions and acting against all better judgment, she intervened. And to do that she had to place her life and body in the hands of two men drunk on newly found power.

"You don't want her. She doesn't know what she's doing, but I'll curl your toes in. That's a fact." It was ridiculous, but she had made up her mind.

Phil smirked. "Fine. Hop in."

Jen climbed aboard the boat without a struggle as her friends begged her not to go. At least she had made the decision, Jen unconvincingly told herself. It was little comfort once the ordeal began.

There was no rescue attempt launched and no sudden arrival of do-gooders as the boat slipped away from the artificial island. Instead, the jackals circled the station about a hundred yards out, close enough that Jen's screams for help easily carried to those left behind. And they could do nothing for her.

Padma and Mary trembled with anger and sorrow while Jackie stayed focused on the task at hand, frantically searching for any type of weapon she could find. But there was nothing useful around. They were defenseless.

The psychos returned after half an hour of sadistic torture, and Phil tossed Jen, used and abused, onto the concrete floor. Then he addressed the women as they tended to their unconscious friend. "We'll be back. And you better have fish waiting for us or someone else is getting the special treatment. Hell, who am I kidding? Somebody's getting the treatment regardless. But without any fish, it's gonna be worse."

Bobby gave them a wink and untied the boat. "Well... bye."

And so the boat left with the two men, one a teacher and the other a janitor, laughing heartily. Soon they would reach loved ones waiting for them with bated breath and smiling faces, eager for stories of adventure and the promise of life-giving food.

Chapter 12
No Rest for the Wicked

A large man named Kyle walked through an Illinois forest with nothing particular on his mind and no agenda to speak of. This day, like many days lately, had been rather uneventful. That is, until a screaming child caught his meager attention. He quietly turned and moved in the direction of the screams with haste. Only it wasn't benevolence or curiosity driving him on. Kyle was infected. And he was one dangerous son of a bitch.

Once remembered for his perpetual smile and gentle demeanor, now he was consumed by hunger and anger, but mostly hunger. The family man and practical joker had been transformed into an unintentional face-eating flesh-ripping terror. Looming six-foot-six and tipping the scales at a ripped two-thirty, Kyle had become an outlier of the deadly variety. The college basketball star and successful business executive had been impressive in life. As a killer, he was even more so.

If anyone was keeping track of stats – and nobody was – Kyle would be ranking somewhere near the top of North America when it came to murders, mayhem, and overall zombie badass-itude. He could rip doors off hinges, snatch a person from halfway up a tree and chase down all but the swiftest of men. He'd overran one small town all by himself, wandering into the back of a town-hall meeting, unnoticed until it was too late, and the panic spiral had begun.

Still, a zombie can't be blamed for its appetite any more than a lion or shark, even one as prolific as Kyle.

And so it was that Kyle's desires and keen sense of hearing brought him directly face to face with a lovable burnout called Smokey.

Smokey had been singing his favorite Grateful Dead song (off-key) in an unsuccessful bid to calm the kid down. He stopped in his tracks. "Heya man," Smokey said at the sight of Kyle before realizing it was a zombie peering at him from the undergrowth. But when Kyle burst from the bushes like a fox after a hare, there was no question about his intentions.

Contending with the squirming and screaming child, Smokey backpedaled and turned to flee, ducking under a low hanging branch at the last second. Kyle didn't see it and wouldn't have cared if he did, and the solid oak bough cracked him good, tearing a chunk of his scalp off in the process. The violent collision slowed him down, but not by much, and soon the muscle-bound monster bounded after his target with renewed vigor. Long legs brought him closer to his prey with every single step, and the noisy child was literally putting him into a frenzy.

Years of toking up while watching cartoons on Adult Swim hadn't left Smokey in prime running shape, but being on the menu was one hell of a motivator. Luckily for him the chase had started when he was almost back to the convent, and before long the walled compound was in sight.

"Open the gate!" Smokey managed to shout between gasps for precious, precious air.

At long last, little Todd finally stopped crying and began to giggle as he bounced around on Smokey's shoulder, thinking it was some sort of game rather than a mad race for their lives.

Sister Katherine was hard of hearing and down to her last eye, the other having been replaced by a crudely painted glass prosthetic. Even so, she'd remained an integral member of the convent, carrying out her duties cheerfully and proficiently. Her one job at the moment was to wait for the return of Charlie and company. So when Smokey came screaming and running across the field at such a rapid pace, she rushed to act. Unfortunately, Sister Katherine's rushing was actually quite slow, and her arthritic fingers, crippled by years of hand-sewing Rosary baubles, could only move so fast.

The stress of the situation caused her to get flustered, and so she stopped in the process of unlocking the gate to say a short prayer. Smokey was almost at the gate now and Kyle was less than a stone's throw behind him. The nun resumed her task with shaking and weak hands. She grasped the latch. It wouldn't move.

Smokey reached the gate and saw the woman fumbling with the latch. He grasped underneath Todd's arms and prepared to chuck him over the eight-foot fence, realizing it was better than the alternative. "Sorry, buddy," he said and began to throw the child, but then the gate opened.

Smokey stopped mid-toss and tumbled onto the ground inside the compound. He spun around and shut the gate as Sister Katherine locked the latch, and the hard-charging zombie slammed into it. Todd was still laughing.

A winded Smokey looked to the nun. "I really need to stop smoking pot. Do you know how to bake brownies?"

Of course, the nun had taken a vow of silence and didn't answer. She patted the child on the head, pointed Smokey towards the front door, and turned to face Kyle. Then Sister Katherine fell to her knees, praying for the zombie's salvation.

Smokey rolled his eyes and walked inside the convent where the Mother Superior was waiting. She grabbed Todd and handed him over to the scarred nun who promptly whisked the now-sleeping child upstairs. "Where are your friends?" Mother Agnes asked.

"No clue. We got separated and... I just don't know." He pulled the bag of supplies from around his shoulder and set it down. "Charlie and Rob have been in some tight spots before. They might turn up."

"And the child?"

"He was an orphan we picked up. I have some diapers and toys for him. Not sure what you're gonna do about milk and stuff."

"We have a cow and the finest fruits and vegetables around," she said, then smiled. "I have to say, I am impressed. That kind of selfless act is a bit surprising from a group that includes your friend Matthew."

"Mathew? Oh, you mean Left-Nut... I mean Lefty. Was he giving you shi—?"

"He has been a bit challenging. At first I thought it was his injury giving him fits, or the painkillers. But after conversing with the man I am confident he's absolutely as advertised. But back to the child."

"Todd."

"He will be well cared for here. Obviously you'll leave him behind when you move on."

Smokey nodded as he thought about Todd's wailing. It would be safer for everyone involved if the child stayed with the gentle flock. Not to mention the crying was getting on his nerves. He remembered the monster from outside. "Oh, and there's one more thing. A huge cannibal, zombie, cavity creep – or whatever you want to call it – is outside. One of the nuns is out there with him right now. You should get her inside. These things, they need more than prayers."

"More than prayers? You should know there's no such thing, and prayers might be exactly what these creatures need. Certainly, the one who gave life to all could restore it to those that have passed, if that is his will."

Smokey was about to delve into one of his favorite topics. "Sorry, but we're not talking about undead zombies here. This is a whole different ball of wax. They're—"

"You might be an expert on zompies, but I happen to know a bit about the scripture. And this situation is hardly novel."

As Mother Agnes pontificated on the various finer points of scripture while Smokey's eyes glazed over, Sister Katherine was putting those points into practice. She silently introduced herself to the man on the other side of the fence, then fell to her knees once more and closed her eye. If there was one thing the eighty-five-year-old could still do as well as any younger person, it was pray. And so she prayed for Kyle the zombie six ways to Sunday. She really gave it to him, hitting all the high notes as well as some lesser-known quotes she'd saved for a special occasion. Minutes later, Sister Katherine opened her eye, confident the prayers had been answered. Kyle was standing right next to her.

In an instant he was upon her, savagely taking hold and tearing into her withered and papery flesh. Lost in her prayers and hard of hearing, Sister Katherine had not noticed Kyle jumping onto the top of the fence and scampering over, and it cost the kindly woman her life.

Kyle plucked Katherine's fake eyeball from its socket and chewed with gusto, shattering teeth and shredding his mouth to a prickly, bloody mush. And he enjoyed every second of it, having no idea the gore was of his own making. Soon, the nun stood up and followed him to the front door, no longer bothered by her sore joints and crippling arthritis.

Sister Francesca, a shy nun from El Salvador, was just going outside to tend to the vegetable garden and didn't even see them approaching. They latched on and feasted in earnest while Francesca opened her mouth in a silent scream. Having dutifully followed her oath of silence for eight years, her vocal cords were not strong enough to register above a whisper, and so the rest of the convent carried on about their business, unaware of the foxes in the henhouse.

The next unlucky lady to enter the buzz saw was Sister Martha, a wheelchair-bound nun that was in the midst of wheeling herself towards the kitchen for dish detail. She saw the bloody mess and frantically tried to turn her chair around, tipping it over in the process. Several bites later and she too was added to the ranks of the infected.

It was at this point in time that Left-Nut hobbled into the entryway looking for more painkillers. "Are those douche nozzles back with my stuff? These pills are starting to wear off and—" he stopped mid-sentence upon seeing the growing puddle of blood on the marble floor. That's when Sister Martha started crawling after him with murder on the mind. "Jesus Christ!" he screamed and hopped away towards the kitchen on one foot, barely keeping ahead of her slobbering mouth.

Hearing the commotion, Smokey and Mother Agnes ran in from the adjoining room and found themselves face to face with Kyle and his growing posse of nightmare nuns.

"Not this fucking guy again," Smokey said as Agnes pulled him into a tiny bathroom, shutting the door before the others could reach them. Their safety was short-lived, however, as bodies began slamming into the wooden door with great force.

Smokey looked around the small room for a weapon and settled for the porcelain lid from the toilet tank. "What? It's either this or the plunger," Smokey said as the door continued to shake from the naughty nuns.

"You won't need either," Mother Agnes said and pointed to the frosted glass window before pushing the panel open. "Sometimes, when God closes a door, he opens a wind—"

Kyle's long arms shot through the opening and yanked Mother Agnes outside in a violent split second. Her zombie converting experiment was over before it began, and now she was on the other team, clamoring for warm sustenance.

Not waiting for Kyle to grab him as well, Smokey decided to take his chances with the hungry nuns instead. He opened the door and shoved one-eyed

Katherine back before slamming the lid down on Sister Francesca's head, shattering it into hundreds of pieces.

Smokey ran past them and bounded up the stairs with the twin terrors in hot pursuit. Where he was going he had no clue, but sticking around wasn't an option anymore.

Luckily for him, Sam appeared at the top of the landing and fired his rifle off, dropping both nuns after missing several times.

"Sweet shooting, partner," Smokey said and grinned. But the expression soon faded as the tall zombie responsible for the bloodbath wandered back through the front door, somehow hungrier than ever.

Sam pulled the trigger and realized he was out of ammo. "Uh oh."

Kyle sprinted up the stairs and chased the two down a long hallway where they found themselves in front of a locked bedroom. They pounded on the door until it opened up, finding the disfigured nun and Todd inside. They shut the door in a hurry, and once more Kyle was left banging on the other side.

Sam and Smokey braced the door with a small bed and waited to see if it would hold. It did, but that didn't stop the zombie on the other side from breaking his hands while hitting it repeatedly. Little Toddy began screaming again, which caused the assault on the door to intensify.

The nun, Sister Katya from Ukraine, tenderly rocked the child back and forth. But he just kept screaming, and Smokey's head began to spin as if he'd taken too many of Julio's magic mushrooms. His friends were most likely dead, he'd gotten a bunch of nuns killed, and they appeared to be trapped. For once, Smokey was devoid of brilliant ideas, and he was scared.

A bloody hand punched through the door and Smokey grabbed a pillow to try to push it back through. A second hand punched through and Sam smacked at it with his empty rifle. Another swing and the beast would be inside.

TATATATATATAT! Machine gun fire rattled down the hallway and the probing arms went limp as blood swiftly streamed underneath the door. Zombie Kyle was no longer hungry.

The survivors heard voices talking excitedly in a strange tongue, and Smokey's heart sank. He had heard that language days earlier, coming from members of the invading army. Smokey and the others were just as trapped as before, maybe even worse.

Smokey grabbed the rifle from Sam. "Sorry, but you should sit this one out. They might spare the women and children, if you're lucky."

"What about you?"

Smokey ignored the question and looked to Katya. "Put a word in for me with the big guy." Of course, like the other nuns, she couldn't talk. He took a deep breath and turned the handle, prepared to go out in a blaze of glory, much like Uncle Russ had.

"All clear?" asked a familiar voice.

Smokey opened the door, not to a hail of gunfire, but to the smiling faces of Rob and Charlie standing with the two North Korean soldiers from the forest. He stepped over the dead body and greeted his friends with a round of hugs before nodding to the Koreans. "Sup dudes?" They nodded back, albeit with little emotion, and walked away to continue securing the sprawling complex.

Rob and Charlie were once again covered in gore and looked exhausted, but they were alive. "I see little Toddy made it," Charlie said and pointed in the direction of the screaming child.

"Yeah, some of the nuns didn't though..." As Smokey's words trailed off, Mother Agnes appeared from around the corner. Her brown robes flowed behind her as she came at them like something from a Victorian horror novel. But she was no supernatural being, and Rob ended her existence with a few blasts from his deadly softball bat.

Smokey pulled the Mother Superior's habit over her destroyed face and stifled his tears. "She was a cool chick."

Charlie nodded. "Where's Left-Nut?"

"No clue," Smokey said with a shrug.

Katya took Todd into a different room and pushed a dresser against the door as the others went to locate their missing friend and any other survivors. After a few minutes they encountered several nuns barricaded in the chapel, but no Left-Nut.

Sam noticed a trail of blood going into the kitchen. Inside, a zombified Sister Martha dragged herself around piles of vegetables and chairs as she came towards them. Rob was once again forced to step up and do what had to be done. It was messy.

Sam gagged and then threw up his meager lunch after witnessing the nun put down in a gruesome, yet humane manner. Embarrassed, he hung his head and slunk to the corner of the room, hoping to disappear into the wall.

"Nothing to be ashamed of," Charlie said. "That's a normal reaction to the craziness going on." He turned to Rob. "And for better or worse, it seems Left-Nut has disappeared. Though I'm sure he'll turn up."

"Like a case of herpes," Rob said and chuckled as he used a dishtowel to wipe the gore off his size eighteen shoe.

One of the overhead cabinets shot open and a person tumbled out, landing on the giant and knocking him backwards. It was Left-Nut.

"About time you ass-munches got back," he said and stood up before noticing his wound had reopened. "Man, I think I, I think I'm gonna..." Left-Nut's eyes fluttered as he fell forward, cracking his head loudly on the floor. A deep gash appeared on his forehead that bled profusely.

Charlie sighed and applied pressure with a kitchen towel, not knowing whether to smile or scowl. "This guy always turns up, like a floater in the gene pool."

At that moment the Koreans walked in, and completely ignored the body, Left-Nut, and the conversation. They scarfed down the blood-covered potatoes scattered about, and it became clear they hadn't eaten in quite some time.

In the past few months, the duo's lot in life had gone from horrible in North Korea to unimaginable under Chinese leadership. Treated as second or even third-class, their kind was used for cannon fodder at every turn. Or, to be more precise, zombie fodder. When the food ran low or their jobs reached completion, the Korean troops were dealt with like vermin. It was this type of cold and calculating style that had the Chinese winning the war handily. But after President Sanders destroyed half of the civilized world in a thermonuclear downpour, the merciless communists could hardly be seen as the war's lone maniacs.

"I take it we're friends now?" Smokey said and tipped his head towards the ravenous soldiers. "What are their names?"

"Not sure," Rob answered with a shrug. He grabbed one of the men by the shoulder. "My name's Rob, what's your name?" The skinny soldier flashed a confused and snaggle-toothed smile, then went back to eating.

"I said, my name's Rob, what's your name?" he asked again, twice as slow and three times as loud. Rob got the same reaction as the first time.

"You know, I don't think it works like that," Charlie said and held back a chuckle. "It looks like we have a bit of a language barrier." Used to communicating with non-English-speaking students during his time substitute teaching, Charlie tried to converse using differing hand gestures and facial expressions. After a short while the soldiers began to grasp what he was getting at.

"Yong Chui," the taller and older of the two men proudly replied and pointed at himself. "Seung Sahn," he continued and gestured to the skinny one who was barely a teenager.

Charlie and company attempted to say the names for a few minutes, but continued to mangle them badly. "All right, this is going nowhere and we have stuff to do." He pointed to Yong Chui. "I'm sorry, but I can't pronounce that properly. So we will call you Ping, and your friend is going to be Pong."

"Doesn't that seem a little racist to anyone?" Smokey asked.

"What would you call them then?" Charlie said.

"How about Rico and Suave?"

"Not happening."

Rob said the first names that came to mind. "Bert and Ernie?"

"Are you kidding me? They'll never be able to correctly pronounce the R's," Smokey said.

Charlie scoffed. "Oh, now who's being racist?"

The Koreans seemed somewhat amused by the conversation. The first soldier stepped forth and pointed to himself. "Ping." He pointed to the younger man. "Pong."

"And there we have it," Charlie said, happy to be done with the matter. And so it was settled. Ping and Pong, two soldiers from North Korea's Special Operation Forces, had joined the gang. What that actually meant was anyone's guess. They came from different corners of the world and their people were now mortal enemies, but each side only drew breath because of the other. With a bond like that, the other considerations paled in comparison. Or so Charlie hoped.

Rob gave his new friends bloody bear hugs and grinned broadly. Ping and Pong humored him and then went back to eating quietly and in a hurry as if they had to fill their bellies before someone would steal their food.

Sam finally got over his embarrassment and rejoined the group. "Why are you guys so happy?" he asked with a furrowed brow. "A lot of good people just got killed here. And you're all still joking and laughing. It's like nothing matters to you guys." Indeed, since joining them, he had found nothing but death following in their wake.

Charlie nodded. "You're right. We've become a bit callous with the whole apocalypse thing going on."

"Not to mention we were assholes before this whole thing got started," Smokey added as an aside.

"Regardless, we should shut up and take care of business. These women deserve a proper burial, not our witty banter. Let's find some shovels," Charlie said, even though he could barely walk, let alone dig graves for the fallen. "This might take a while."

Chapter 13
Dangerous Liaisons

Phil piloted the boat towards the water pumping station while Bobby paced back and forth, hardly able to contain his excitement. It had been a week since they found the isolated spot and the women trapped there, and it was all the creeps could think about.

The former high school employees hadn't always been of such low character, but violence and scarcity has a way of changing men to their very cores. With law enforcement a thing of the past, these guys would only get worse. As their actions spiraled out of control one heinous deed at a time, moral relativism became more than just a vocabulary word from one of Bobby's boring AP philosophy classes.

The pair had waited impatiently for the opportunity to slip away from their clueless families, and it had finally arrived. Running low on food meant a supply run was necessary, but food was far from either of their fevered minds as they dropped anchor and tied off once again.

By now Jackie and her friends had even less food since theirs had been taken, and they now relied on whatever seafood Mary could pull from the lake. Some days they didn't eat at all.

Even worse was the thought that the two men could show up at any moment and once again steal what little peace they had left in a world gone mad. And without enough food to feed themselves, they had none to spare for the Lake Shore pirates. This would give the men another convenient excuse to fuel their brutality – not that they needed any.

Now the moment the women had dreaded had arrived as Phil and Bobby stepped cautiously onto the concrete floor. They didn't have the element of surprise this time, but the moon was partially obscured by thick cloud cover, and so it was a rather dark night. The wind was picking up and lightning sparked in the distance as Phil looked around for any signs of their intended victims. Nada. What he did find was a five-gallon bucket conspicuously placed out in the open. He kicked it over and fish heads slid over the ground in all directions.

"You stupid bitches." Phil looked at his partner in crime and grinned. "That's not the only head we're gonna be getting tonight."

"Good one," Bobby said with a laugh. The teacher was out of his element on the lake and had relied on the sketchy night shift janitor to survive in the beginning. But if their ways parted, Bobby had quietly learned everything he needed to know for the future.

Phil started walking towards the main building but stopped in his tracks with his foot in midair. He had almost stepped on a bunch of rusty nails scattered around like caltrops. Weeks before, puncture wounds like that would have been a painful mistake. But now, without access to medical care, that mistake could prove as deadly as a gunshot.

The men stepped around the hazard while joking about the women's incompetence. But they didn't find it funny when a three-ton load of steel pipes dropped on them from above and smashed their bones like fine china. It turned out that violence and scarcity has a way of changing women to their very cores as well. In this case, it changed them into survivors.

Jackie opened the door to the crane and ran to the fallen men, taking their pistols away in a flash as her friends burst from hiding spots nearby, brandishing improvised weapons. They didn't need them. Phil the janitor had been killed instantly under the load of metal and Bobby was left horribly mangled. He screamed in agony as Jackie searched him for anything of value, and then dragged his ruined body to the edge of the platform.

"Please, I have kids," Bobby managed to sputter out through the blood streaming from his mouth.

"You don't have anything but regret," Jackie said and stepped back.

At that point, Jen, still bruised and battered from her rough treatment a week earlier, came forward and looked into the dying man's eyes. There was one final thing she had left to say.

"Well, bye."

With that, Jen kicked hard and Bobby rolled into the water with a splash, vanishing beneath the waves as if he'd never existed.

*   *   *

The fishing boat was running on empty as it cruised towards the south end of the lake in near darkness. Jackie did her best to avoid the bloated corpses bobbing up and down in the water, but still hit them from time to time. Each loud thump of a floater was a reminder of what they were about to face on dry land.

At that same moment in the city, Charlie and his friends were arguing over cat food and the smell of Rob's feet, and Jen's fiancé, Blake, was still alive and as pompous as ever. But the two groups might as well have been worlds apart, separated by a million bloodthirsty creatures and the dense fog of disaster.

The choppy water was making Mary sick, and she did her best not throw up as cold spray hit them continuous‐ly. They had no clue where their next meal was coming from and she couldn't risk losing what little protein was left in her stomach. She sat down and closed her eyes. "Any idea how much farther?" she asked, her mouth watering.

"Not far," Jackie said. "We'll do this just like we talked about. Go as far south as we can and put up anchor a good distance out. I'll swim in and find us a car. From there we head to the boonies and play it by ear."

It sounded like a reasonable enough plan when Jackie said it out loud, but there were a lot of assumptions she was making and plenty of ways things could go to shit at Mach speed. Even so, Mary trusted her completely. The straight-talking businesswoman hadn't failed her yet, and things were looking up after getting off the station.

The boat shook violently as it crashed into more bodies and Mary finally succumbed, puking onto the floor as Padma held her brown hair aloft. "See, there's land just ahead," Padma said, then turned to Jen. "You okay? You've been awful quiet."

"Yep. Just dandy." Jen had been looking at the wallet on the floor of the boat ever since they had gotten in.

She knew she shouldn't care, but there it was, beckoning at her to take a peek. Finally she ripped it open as the boat neared the shoreline. Inside was Bobby's driver's license. Bobby Bradford of Michigan City, to be more precise.

The flip side was more interesting, though, and that's what Jen was curious about. There was a photo of a man, standing with his family, dressed in their Sunday's finest. Bobby had a huge smile on his face, as did his wife and two rosy-cheeked daughters. It was clear they were crazy about him and Jen could picture the photogenic bunch frantically worried about his whereabouts. Would they survive without their closet psychopath? She didn't care.

Jen tossed the wallet into the water where it floated for a moment and then, like Bobby himself, disappeared under the surf.

Chapter 14
Enter the Dragon

Two weeks had passed since the mayhem at the nun-nery and Left-Nut had at long last healed enough to travel, much to the delight of all the remaining nuns he had been pestering. Over that period Charlie and friends filled their bellies with actual food, slept in beds, and generally forgot about their troubles for a time. But as comfortable as their sanctuary was, Charlie was eager to head back to the wastelands beyond the fence. He had a budding family to find, made up of his pregnant girlfriend and adopted son, and with every day that passed they felt less and less real.

So as the sun rose one morning, the gang packed up and said their goodbyes to the group of speechless nuns and the screaming baby they were leaving behind. By the look on the elderly women's faces, they were just fine with it.

As the group neared the gate, one of the nuns ran to them and handed over a piece of paper. It was the woman named Katya – or Scarface, as the guys called her behind her back.

"Sorry, but you're not coming with us," Charlie said and handed the paper back to the nun, noticing a small tattoo of a flower on her hand. "It's too dangerous, and this note stuff just isn't going to work. We all have to pull our weight and look out for each other. If you see a zombie sneaking up and you can't shout a warning, well that's gonna get us all killed. And we're already doing a pretty good job of that."

Rob appeared agitated. "I think she should come. We could always use an extra pair of hands, and she knows how to cook." And there was the reason. He was a mountain of consistency.

Charlie believed he had a way out. "All right, she can come. If she's willing to talk."

Katya looked at her feet and took a deep breath. Regretfully, she nodded her head. "Okay," she said, in a barely audible tone. The nun hadn't spoken in quite a while and her vocal cords were in need of exercise. More importantly, she had just broken her vow of silence. But Katya believed God wanted her to join these men who were so desperately in need of guidance. Not to mention the convent was slowly but surely driving her insane with boredom.

Surprised, Charlie smiled. "I guess that's a start then. Keep practicing." He turned to Rob. "This is on you, so she's under your protection. Keep her safe and show her how to defend herself."

"No problem," Rob said. He grabbed one of the shovels from the nearby garden and handed it to his new friend. "Stay close to me and aim for the head when you can. If they bite you it's all over, so don't let that happen. And most importantly, stay away from Left-Nut."

Katya nodded before donning a backpack and hugging several of the less dour nuns goodbye. Then she pinched little Todd's angry face and turned to leave with the others. The gate closed behind them and nobody looked back as the padlock snapped into place. Katya took a deep breath and smelled the freedom of the open road. Then Rob farted.

"Woops. That cabbage is still doing a number on me. Can't say I'll miss it."

Katya held in a smile – and her breath – and walked a bit farther away from her protector. It wasn't long before she noticed Left-Nut was following closely behind. Or, more specifically, just her behind.

"Move it," she rasped and cleared her throat. This was a different lifestyle indeed, and they hadn't even gone a hundred yards yet.

And so Katya's new life of adventure began as they traveled by foot through a countryside she'd lived next to for years but had never seen. The morning went by without much excitement as Charlie talked to Sam about sports and Smokey babbled on about his favorite TV shows, neither of which Katya had any clue about. Still, she enjoyed the company and the sound of human voices, even if Rob had to shoo Left-Nut away from time to time.

She didn't know it, but the reason the morning had gone by so smoothly was due to the Koreans. Ping and Pong had forged ahead to scout for the group and had already dealt with several random zombies in a discreet and efficient manner. Obviously they had been a worthy addition to the gang. It remained to be seen if Katya would be the same.

After several hours of hiking under a cloudy sky, Charlie decided it was time for a quick break and stopped them by the edge of the forest. The group huddled together into a protective circle while sipping from water bottles. Katya produced a crusty loaf of bread from her pack and it was quickly passed around.

"I baked this, today," she said with effort.

"Thanks," Charlie said. "You sound better already. Now if we only knew what the hell they were saying, we'd be in business," he added while pointing to one of the Koreans coming back from across the next field.

"I might be able to talk to them," Left-Nut said casually between chews. "Wow, this bread is drier than an old lady's—"

"Don't you think that might have been important to know?" Charlie asked while forming a fist. This was something that happened every time he talked to his white-haired frenemy.

"You never asked," Left-Nut said. "And to be honest, my Korean's a little shaky. I met this hot chick from Seoul while playing in a StarCraft tournament online. I wanted to bang her so bad but then I found out she was only sixteen... so then I really wanted to bang her. Never did, though. Such a shame."

Smokey looked absolutely disgusted. "Not cool, man. But leaving your creepiness factor aside for a moment, it's worth a shot. Let her rip."

Left-Nut smiled at Pong and tried to communicate. This amounted to him asking if "Pong's sweater nipples were hungry apple."

Pong arched an eyebrow, obviously baffled by the string of what resembled authentic frontier gibberish. "Mo·na·ra·dǔt·kke·ssǒ·yo," he replied, clearly confused.

Left-Nut looked at Charlie. "See, now we're making progress. I asked him if he had a sister and he said he would love for me to meet her."

"Damn it, just ask him if they plan on sticking around with us. Every time they go off we don't know if they're coming back or not."

"Fine, fine. That's out of my range, but I'll get serious." He turned back to Pong. "Chǒ·nǔn han·gung·mal chal·mo·t'ae·yo," he said, admitting that his Korean was bad. The pronunciation was way off, but Pong understood. Progress.

The soldier nodded with a smile and pulled him aside so the two could set about learning each other's language in earnest. It was an odd pair for sure – a North Korean trained for asymmetric warfare and an American lowlife skilled in the arts of douchebaggery – but these were odd times.

While they worked on the fundamentals, Charlie told Katya of their plans. They had about a hundred miles to go before reaching their destination, and that was as the crow flies. Dealing with the terrain while avoiding cannibals and the Chinese army could add plenty of extra

116

ground to cover. "We just have to keep putting one foot in front of the other and keep our eyes peeled. Plus, no more delays would be nice," he added while casting a glance in Left-Nut's direction.

After fifteen minutes the group got back at it, now rehydrated and ready to rock. They crossed the next empty field in high spirits as Big Rob quietly serenaded everyone with an amazing rendition of the Elvis classic "Don't Be Cruel." Even Pong was humming along, though he had no clue what the words meant.

As they prepared to enter the next wooded patch, the other Korean popped out from the trees and was in an unmistakably agitated state. "Tta-ra o-se-yo!" he exclaimed, motioning them to follow.

Everyone gripped their weapons tightly as they followed close behind, the language barrier adding an extra layer of worry. Nobody was prepared for the sight that greeted them inside the forest.

Bodies. Lots of them. Everyone save Katya had already seen their fair share of the dead, but this was something different entirely. Some were skeletal, others fresh, but all had been impaled on crudely carved wooden stakes that protruded from the ground.

"This isn't good," Rob said as he swatted away a large crow that had been pecking at a woman's putrid eyeball.

Katya grasped her rosary and began saying as many prayers as she could, fighting through the pain that each word caused her.

"Were they zombies or people?" Sam asked as he looked at the body of a red-haired girl about his age. She could have been his sister.

"Does it matter?" Left-Nut asked.

"I think so, yes," the boy answered.

Smokey checked a few of the bodies. "Yep, they all have bite marks. Whoever did this is a badass."

"No, whoever did this is mucho loco," Charlie said. "We're talking Dahmer level here. Better keep moving."

117

Katya said a few more prayers and then they hurried from the macabre setting. Minutes later the group arrived near the edge of the forest where they came upon a small farmstead. A few scrawny head of cattle milled about behind a wooden fence as dozens of chickens foraged for insects in the tall grass.

A tall man opened the gate to gather the chickens and then stopped, looking in their direction. He was built like Hercules and his haircut was very distinct, sort of a hybrid mullet with the sides shaved off. Rob wasted no time and charged from their hidden position with the war cry of a fanatic on his lips. Rather than bash the man's brains on the spot, however, Rob tossed his bat aside and collided with him instead, taking the guy down hard.

The chickens fluttered around in a panic as the two titans fought for position. With much effort, Rob was able to stay on top and began to rain blows down on his adversary. The old ground and pound.

But the pummeled man somehow pulled a Rambo-style knife from his belt and shoved it upwards at Rob's thick neck. The sound of automatic gunfire made him stop mid slash, however, and he dropped the weapon to the ground.

Pong lowered his weapon and Charlie pulled Big Rob back. Now was his chance to recognize the wounded mystery man. His jaw dropped at the revelation. It was Vladimir. The Dragon. Draganov. World Champion fighter and all-around villain.

"You ruined my life you piece of shit," Rob said as he gasped for air and contemplated another go of it.

Vladimir was also fighting for breath, but he had a dumb smile on his face at the same time.

"Unfortunate? Yes, but are not all lives ruined?" He spit a mouthful of bloody teeth onto the ground. "Nice to see you, too."

"Fuck off."

An elderly man and woman tentatively walked towards the group, carrying pitchforks and speaking a Russian-sounding language. Vlad waved at them to back off. "Besides, not my fault. Owner set you up. Owner set me up when problems with skanks began. We peas in pod."

"No, we aren't anything alike," Rob said and continued to glare at him with murder on his mind.

Charlie intervened at just the right moment to prevent further meathead mayhem. "Why don't you bring up the rear for a few and cool off?" he suggested to Rob.

Rob nodded and sulked off as the others scanned the premises for danger. They were very close to the impaled bodies, after all. Charlie struck a conciliatory tone. "Look, we're just passing through on our way to Cantonville. Obviously Rob was surprised at seeing you, and the fight was unfortunate. Sorry."

"Still many miles to Cantonville," Vlad replied as he sized up the group. "Very dangerous miles."

"That's for us to worry about," Charlie said.

"Headed to base there?" Vlad asked.

"None of your business. Again, sorry for Rob blasting you in the face thirty times, and goodbye."

"Don't be so hasty. We off on wrong ankle with scuffle, but that is no biggie." The Bulgarian's broken English was reminiscent of Vidu's halting speech and just as irritating.

Charlie sighed. "I don't have time to beat around the bush. What do you want? In one sentence."

"Direct approach. I like that—"

"That's it, we're going."

"Fine, fine. Take me with you," Vlad said, a hint of desperation creeping into his voice.

Rob came charging back. "No fucking way he's coming with us. The guy's a rapist."

"Not guilty, bitch."

"Like you didn't pay off a juror?"

Vladimir failed to contest Rob on that point. "Not matter. Vlad innocent anyways."

Charlie stepped between the two giants. "I'd swear you guys used to date. Anyways, let's crank the testosterone down a notch, both of you." He turned to Vlad. "Why would we want to take you along?"

Vlad retrieved the long knife from his belt and threw it at a wooden post fifteen yards away, burying it to the hilt. "Was Bulgarian special forces ten years. Trained to kill, live off land, and travel undetected. All things needed to get to Cantonville. Plus, Vlad has chickens. Armies march faster on full bellies."

Rob let his guard down ever so slightly when food was mentioned while Charlie ground his teeth, pondering the offer. For sure, Vladimir could prove to be a deadly, albeit annoying, ally. On the other hand, he was a known psychopath with extremely violent tendencies and a total disregard for authority.

So basically, Vlad was no different than half of the rag-tag band of survivors.

Charlie pointed to the aged couple. "And you're okay with leaving your parents here, defenseless?"

"That Vlad's mother, but not Vlad's father. Father was great warrior, died in battle with communists. That is uncle. The coward is good for cleaning chicken coop and little else."

"Regardless, I mean... there's a bunch of bodies on spikes not far from here, not to mention the zombies and the Chinese soldiers," Charlie pressed.

"Tossing crazies on spikes great way to stay in shape. Also keeps, how you say, looky-loos away from farm. Anyways, Vlad wanted to protect mother when world went topsy-turvy. But she driving crazy with chores." He pointed to his barrel chest. "World champion three years. Now? Castrate pigs, shovel shit, feed chickens. No more." He walked over to the post to recover his knife. "Have heard of Spartacus? Was born in Bulgaria. Draganov lore

120

claims him as ancestor. Many others in family honored fighters, too. To be like them, Vlad must die in glorious battle."

Charlie arched an eyebrow. "And?"

"And Vlad not find glorious battle at Bumfuck chicken farm."

At least they knew what maniac was responsible for the impaled zombies and why Vlad so desperately wanted to join them.

"Okay, we're gonna talk this over so give us a minute," Charlie said.

"Take time."

The group huddled up. Currently sober and unimpaired by any other mind-altering substances, they were at least thinking clearly.

Rob spoke first. "No. No effing way," he said quietly, almost in a growl. "Vlad can't be trusted."

"If he can throw a zombie onto a spike as cross-training, the dude has mad skills. Sorry bro," Smokey said. "He could help us for sure."

Sam nodded in agreement. "I saw him on television. The guy can fight. And no offense to Miss Katya, but after all those vegetables, meat sounds good."

"I think I actually agree with the pledge. I want some damned chicken," Left-Nut said with his mouth watering at the thought. "Plus he can kick Rob's big ass. So for me it's a win-win."

"He cheated," Rob mumbled as the harsh realization set in that, yes, the apocalypse could get even worse. The man that had ruined Rob's real life would once again become a thorn in his side.

"Katya?" Charlie said. "He has a bad history with women. Like, Chris Brown bad."

"I have no idea who that is, but I trust you to make the right decision," she said.

Charlie placed his hand on Rob's shoulder. It was settled. "Sorry, but we can't let our personal vendettas get in the way of survival. If we did, Left-Nut would be dead by now. So we'll keep him on a tight leash, and if he doesn't fit in, we send him packing. Consider it a test drive."

"Big mistake," Rob said.

"Maybe so," Charlie said, more to himself as the huddle dispersed. "Vlad, grab that chicken, pack your gear and say your goodbyes. You're coming with us. Just don't forget, you pull any scandalous maneuvers and you're on your own."

Vlad retrieved some items from the farmhouse and then hugged his crying mother while totally ignoring his uncle. Moments later he led the growing group of misfits into the next forest beyond the farm.

"Is woman spoken for?" Vlad said to nobody in particular. Katya turned to give him a dirty look and Vlad saw her scar for the first time. "Whoa, never mind. Has body of gymnast and face of burnt *patatnik*." He smacked Left-Nut's arm. "Gives me... how you say opposite of hard-on? Soft-off?"

Left-Nut grinned. "Vladimir, I think this might be the beginning of a beautiful friendship."

"Probably, you both have the personality of cold hotdog water," Charlie said, immediately second guessing his decision. "Now, less chatting and more walking. We have a lot of miles to cover today. And crack open that basket of chicken."

Chapter 15
It's Complicated

The summer had been a hard one for the girls, and they were thankful it was finally coming to a close. Modern living had left their bodies unaccustomed to the realities of hot weather, and a cool breeze that particular night had been welcome indeed. But lower temperatures would not solve all their problems.

Jackie worked her hand axe back and forth before it ultimately popped out of a dead man's skull with a plopping sound. She wiped the blade off on dry grass and breathed a sigh of relief. "That was a close one."

"Tell me about it," Padma said as she rose to her feet and brushed dirt off her scraped knees. "Thanks. I didn't see him coming."

"It's way too dark out here. We need to find somewhere to hide for the night, and soon. There are just too many biters out here." Jackie's last comment was a bit of an understatement as the forest seemed to be crawling with zombies for no apparent reason. Even worse, the light of the full moon meant their movements could be easily detected by the sharp-eyed maniacs.

"Maybe we could check the road again?" Jen said. "There could be a car with tinted windows or something. I'd even sleep under one right now. Or even in the trunk."

Jackie nodded. "Okay. Let's shadow the highway for a bit. If anyone sees trouble, though, it's right back into the woods."

The group of women had been nomads for months, roving from one location to the next, pilfering food and supplies while trying to stay ahead of whatever threats lurked nearby. Their first few weeks had been spent hiding in an abandoned sub-division while eking out a meager existence on wild berries, bugs, and rainwater. But they had slowly wasted away, and Jackie was forced to lead them into the unfamiliar lands southwest of the city. From there they had been driven on by empty stomachs, both their own and by those of their mindless adversaries.

For the most part they'd survived using stealth and patience. After being on the move for fourteen hours straight, though, the latter was running in short supply. They bypassed several abandoned trucks and a tipped-over RV, and found what they were looking for. Not far ahead was a large van with expensive rims and tinted windows.

"Looks like a rape van," Mary said, then bit her lip, expecting some unkind words in response to the gaffe.

Jen calmly stared ahead, emotionless. "No, it does. But it's just what we need. My blisters are killing me and I can't keep my eyes open. Are we ready?"

They were, and the four friends burst from the cover of the scrub trees and rapidly made their way through the overgrown weeds surrounding the highway.

Exposed and clearly visible under the ample moonlight, this was an enormous risk for a group more comfortable playing it safe. But sometimes it paid to go against your own ground rules.

This was not one of those times. The doors were locked and Mary yanked in futility on the handle. Which is when the car alarm turned on.

"Shit, back to the woods," Jackie said as the loud alarm faded away with the last of the car's battery.

Padma held her hand up. "Hold on. Maybe it's okay?"

It wasn't. Scores of infected bolted towards them from farther down the road as well as from the tree line, scuttling towards them like ants joining a picnic.

There were definitely too many to fight off with handheld weapons, and the women were malnourished and in no shape for a pitched battle anyway. This left only one option.

"Follow me," Jackie said as she took off straight down the middle of the road.

A quarter of a mile later and the women were already tiring, with Jen in particular lagging behind. Jackie opened the door of a truck they'd seen earlier and looked for keys. Nothing. She ran to the next one, and again came up empty.

"Climb onto the mobile home," Padma said between pants, realizing Jen was about to faint. As they prepared to scale the tipped Winnebago and engage in a brutal last stand, something in the distance caught all of their attention. Headlights. And they were approaching.

"Screw it, run to the lights!" Jackie said forcefully.

"Are you sure?" Jen asked, lingering briefly.

Jackie tugged at her hesitating friend's arm. "We don't have a choice."

"But what if it's somebody like before?"

"You stay, you die," Jackie said stone-faced. And so the four ran towards the mystery vehicle, unsure of who was driving it or what their intentions were. At this point it didn't matter as fifteen very hungry cannibals sprinted after them. Some had been hobbled by injuries and left a bloody trail in their wake, but others were in peak physical condition. The same could not be said for the emaciated group of survivors.

However, the outcome of this chase would not be decided by how fast the runners were going, but by the speed of the incoming vehicle, which turned out to be a semi. And it was hauling ass.

Mary jumped up and down while waving her arms as the truck approached in a hurry. "It's not slowing."

In fact, it was speeding up, swerving and heading directly at them. The driver honked his horn loudly and, at the last second, cut to the right while locking up the brakes. On instincts the women hit the pavement as the semi jackknifed and its trailer flew forward with squealing tires and burning rubber. Caught unaware, the zombies were completely decimated by the high-risk maneuver of the lunatic behind the wheel.

Jackie and the others climbed out from beneath the trailer and peered up at the driver's side of the cab as the window rolled down. The song "Radar Love" resounded from an expensive stereo system while a lit cigarette butt flew forth like a tracer round in the night. The song quieted. Next, a man with a mullet stuck his head out, grinning oddly as he lingered on Jackie's supple legs for an excruciatingly protracted amount of time.

"Aren't you just a tall drink of hot chocolate," the man said with a twang. "The name's Russell Yitzhak Kaminsky."

"Wait, you're Jewish?" Trent asked from the passenger seat.

"Wasn't it obvious?" Russ said as he batted his disturbing eyes at the women. "Anyways, I'm single, willing to mingle." They stared at him blankly. "You know, all alone and ready to bone?"

The world's sole Jewish redneck zombie-hybrid had saved their lives. He was also drunk, dressed like a pirate, and had a raccoon (in a similar outfit) perched on his shoulder. But to the women, at that moment, he might as well have been a shirtless Brad Pitt riding in on Shadowfax while bottle-feeding a baby tiger.

Except for Jen, who recognized her fiancés "eccentric" uncle in an instant. Ignoring the smashed bodies in the road, her face lit up as she approached the truck. "Oh my God! Russ, I can't believe it's you!"

Trent had exited from the other side and walked around to make sure no zombies were pulling a Jason Voorhees. Once face to face with Jen, her smile grew even wider. "And Trent. I never thought I'd be happy to see you. So where's Blake?"

Awkward. The cop opened his mouth but couldn't vocalize the harsh reality that Blake had been killed by an injection of spoiled insulin. However, his non-answer was enough, and Jen collapsed as the roller-coaster ride of emotions finally overwhelmed her. Mary and Padma comforted her as Jackie sized up the newcomers.

It had been several days since Trent, Russ, and Marquell had emerged from the cavernous tunnels, and much had happened since then. They'd punched, kicked and choked each other numerous times while surviving one harebrained scheme after another. They'd traded jokes, recipes, threats, and insults including words like "bumpkinbilly," "butt slug," "bacon-bastard," and so forth and so on. Russ had even driven off without the others once before coming back two hours later, drunker than David Hasselhoff on vacation. But, as often happens in life or death situations like these, strange bonds of brotherhood can form and the mismatched group had reached a bit of a détente for the moment. Not that Russ or Trent knew what that meant.

Russ had even made Marquell laugh a few times – on the inside at least – and that was a rare thing indeed. Sure, Marquell still had the passing desire to murder Trent every few hours, but not any more than Charlie had while living with him in the apartment.

For now they had an open road in front of them, a handful of attractive women in their presence, and some dead zombies to plunder. Things were looking up.

Jackie approached as the trio searched several dismembered corpses. "My boyfriend was with you the night before it all went down, at the bachelor party. Bruce?"

Trent sighed loudly, wondering why he always had to be the bearer of bad news. "Sorry. He was alive until just a few days ago. The Chinese came from nowhere..."

Jackie nodded. "At least I know. And he's not out there hurting people. That's a positive."

"Nice!" Russ said as he pulled a small flask from a pair of bloody jeans. He tipped the metal container and drained its contents before even checking to see what it was, swishing the liquid around like mouthwash. "Charcoal-filtered scotch. Wasn't expecting that."

"What are you hauling?" Jackie asked, trying to glean any useful information she could. They had been burned by supposed rescuers once already and she was determined not to repeat the mistake. Unfortunately, it was Russ that decided to answer her. In great detail.

"Little lady, right now we're pulling half a load of freight from Adam and Steve, the world's premier source of gay sex toys. We've got butt plugs, double-sided dongs, pocket rockets, and some freaky shit that even I haven't seen before. And that's saying something because I have done some messed up stuff in my life. One time I was with my landlord's wife, and we had a stapler and this bottle of hot sauce—"

"I get the picture," Jackie said, visibly growing uncomfortable. She introduced her group and then thanked the men for their assistance. "If you could help us find a working vehicle, well, that would be great." Despite their good deed, Jackie had decided it would be best to part ways, and soon. She was nothing if not rational.

"Sure thing," Russ said and turned to the doctor. "Padma, isn't that the chick in *Star Wars*? Not the real *Star Wars* but the one with that dumbass Jafar Binks fella."

"I haven't the slightest clue what you're talking about, but would you mind backing up?" Padma said as she noticed his odd mannerisms and weirdly tinted green eyes. Then she detected Russ's missing fingers and apparent lack of pain as he scratched his scraggly salt and pepper beard. She motioned for her friends to step away. "What's going on here? Something's not right with

128

this man."

"No shit," Trent said and received four very dirty looks. He raised his hands in deference. "It's complicated. Well, actually it's not. He's a zombie, but he's our zombie. Unless he sobers up."

"That ain't happening," Russ said and went back to searching the dead as Elvis scampered down and sniffed at a severed foot in the road.

"Or if you get seriously injured he'll turn on you like a buster. Rest in peace, homie." Marquell threw a few gang symbols up in remembrance of his fallen friend. He had come to the realization that Ace Kool would have died anyway, but it did not lessen the blow.

Padma's interest was piqued by the story. "So he's got the same desires and urges as the other cannibals running around, but for some reason he kept his mind?"

"What he had for one, anyway," Trent replied.

"Strange, but fascinating," Padma said as her impressive intellect worked in many different directions. "It appears he's some type of carrier, like a modern day Typhoid Mary. Have you thought about taking him somewhere to get tested? This could be a breakthrough."

"I don't know who the fuck Typhoon Mary is, I was a gym major," Trent said. "Ask me how to set up a kickball tournament though and I'm all over it." He could be charming when he wanted to be, and with the sudden arrival of several attractive women, he wanted to be so in a bad way. "But to answer your question, yes, we are trying to take him somewhere. There's a military base near Cantonville, and some of our other friends might be there already."

The information was a blockbuster in that it gave the women the slightest bit of hope, which was something they had been sorely lacking. They walked away for a moment to plot their course.

"Ladies, any thoughts?" Padma said. "Should we go with them? There is strength in numbers, and if that

129

guy's the cure to this madness then we should help get him to his destination." She looked to Jen. "But can they be trusted?"

Jen shrugged. "Russ was Blake's uncle and I've known him for years. Sure he's a turd, but he was harmless. Then again that was before he got turned into a zombie or whatever. And Trent's always been an asshole. I never met the other guy."

"So?" Padma said.

"I need to sleep. We can always change our minds later."

Jackie looked to Mary. "What do you think?"

Mary still wasn't used to people asking her opinion about anything, and it caught her off guard every time. "I trust Jen's judgment," she said.

"That's it then." Jackie turned to the men. "If it's all right with you, we'd like to join up and head to that base together."

The men smiled in unison, tripping over themselves to be the first to agree. It was amazing what women could do to them, even half-starved ones at that.

Jackie wasn't finished. "Just understand that we won't be putting up with any funny business. The last men that tangled with us ended up regretting it. In a big way."

Trent nodded. "No problem. We've got half a tank of gas and we're barely a few hours away. You girls can sleep in the trailer, and by the time you wake up we'll be home free." He grinned. "Now, if you choose to reward us after saving you and the world, well I won't complain."

Jackie laughed at his hubris. "Get us there first. And I'm riding up front."

"Sure thing. We'll just toss out some of the junk inside to make room for the others. Marquell, a little help?"

They headed towards the back and passed a detailed painting on the side of the cab that showed a horse rider jumping through a ring of fire. The previous owner had been known as "The Flaming Cowboy" for surviving numerous car bombs in Iraq, but he hadn't lasted ten minutes into the apocalypse. It just went to show that when it's your time to go, you go.

"I call dibs on the black chick," Trent whispered to Marquell. "Non-negotiable."

"Bullshit," Marquell whispered in reply. He ignored a pair of brass truck nuts dangling underneath the license plate and unlocked the door to the trailer, shoving it upwards. Some of the raunchy freight had shifted during Russ's stunt and tumbled onto the ground. One of the packages began buzzing loudly.

Trent chuckled at the inappropriate pile of novelties, but then his face turned pale and he grew still. Standing back a few feet into the shadows was a man with a gun and a bowler hat.

Xavier McDaniels, last of the Gutter Punks, psychopath, and all around dickhead had been stowed away like the yeti in Russ's favorite movie, *Big Trouble in Little China*. Xavier grinned but didn't say a word. His gun talked for him as he fired several times into the group at point blank range.

Trent knew what he should do. He knew what he must do. And for the first time in his life, he actually did it. Several bullets struck him as he jumped in front of Jackie and her friends. Whether it was guilt over his past actions or his blossoming heart, the cop had stepped up in a big way. But he paid dearly for it, and now writhed in agony on the ground.

Unfortunately Trent's bulky body had not stopped all the bullets, and Jen lay dead next to him with a gunshot wound to the temple. Painless and quick. It was her time to go.

Xavier jumped down from the trailer while keeping his gun pointed at the others, prepared to execute them one by one. He'd been hiding inside for days, dying of thirst, plotting his revenge, and waiting for someone to eventually unlock the door.

Long seconds passed and he still hadn't spoken a word, enjoying the look of terror on his surprised victims' faces. Having gloated enough, Xavier aimed at Trent's chest to finish him off.

However, before he could pull the trigger, one of the crushed zombies – or one half of a crushed zombie to be precise – reached out from underneath the truck and grabbed his leg. Panicking, Xavier fired several times into the zombie's skull and kicked the dead beast away.

Marquell rushed forward but Xavier whirled and pointed the gun directly at his face, stopping the man in his tracks. The Gutter Punk didn't fire though. He'd lost track of how many shots were left, and if he ran out the angry group was sure to beat him to death. Xavier instead stepped sideways and grabbed the first woman within arm's reach. It was Mary.

The others tensed up even further, as if ready to charge. He needed a plan, and quick. Xavier knew he couldn't drive a big rig, and so it was off to the forest with his hostage in tow. He backed up, clutching Mary tightly with the gun pressed firmly to her spine.

"The minute I see one of you assholes following me, she's the first to die." He nodded to Trent. "I'll see you in hell. It looks like you'll be waiting for me." But Trent had already passed out from pain and blood loss.

Xavier walked backwards for several yards and then dragged Mary off towards the forest. They disappeared a moment later as the others tried to stop Trent's bleeding and argued about what to do.

Jackie pushed Jen's lifeless eyes shut. "We need to go get Mary," she said, steeling her nerves. "We can't just leave her with that murderer. She wouldn't do that to us."

Surprisingly, Padma dissented. "But if he sees us he'll kill her on the spot. I don't know if there's much that we can do about that. Besides, the woods are still crawling with the hungry ones."

Jackie shook her head while clutching her axe furiously. "We have to try."

"This man is seriously hurt, but thankfully the bullets went clean through," Padma said, turning back to Trent. "Still, it's imperative to get these wounds closed up ASAP. I can do it, but it will take proper tools. We need to find a hospital."

Russ had staggered back to the action moments earlier and saw Trent's gaping injuries and Jen's prone body. "Aw, fuck it," he said sadly. Then his mouth started to water and his stomach growled. He turned around after tossing his pirate shirt to Padma for a bandage.

Underneath the costume was what one would expect: a stained white t-shirt with an amateurish tribal tattoo peeking out from the neckline. In many ways, the man broke the mold. But in others he fit the usual stereotypes down to a T.

"Put him in the back of the trailer and I'll get us to a hospital. I know a shortcut."

Chapter 16
Fatso

To say that Big Rob had been pouting all morning would be a vast understatement. He had even almost sulked his way through lunch. Almost. But after wolfing down some of Vlad's free-range fried chicken, he went right back to giving his nemesis the stink eye while bringing up the rear.

It was still clearly painful for Katya to talk, but she was determined to do her part for the group. At the moment, that meant cheering up her protector and offering some heartfelt advice. She timidly touched his shoulder. "There are not many people left. The ones that are must be left for a reason. Trust in that."

Rob wanted to believe his new friend and could see she was sincere, but his anger and resentment levels were too strong for kind words to overcome. "You don't understand, Katya. My whole life has been shit. Sorry, I meant poop. And for one moment it looked like Big Rob was gonna come out on top. I was fighting for a world title, and my dreams were within reach. And Vlad, he took it from me. Made me an even bigger joke than I already was. I still have nightmares about that night. Just looking at him makes me want to throw up."

Katya was undeterred by Rob's reaction and the fact that every word she spoke physically hurt. "If things were different, would you be here right now? With loved ones like Charlie, and yes, even Left-Nut?"

"I guess not," Rob said begrudgingly. "Who knows where I would have ended up, but I sure would have been too busy for Blake's bachelor party. I know that for damned sure."

"So maybe it worked out for best? All have roles to play, and yours might be just beginning. Possibly Vlad's too?"

"Sure."

"What's that smell?" she asked, the flawless side of her face wrinkling in displeasure as the scarred side remained motionless.

"Sorry, I beefed," Rob said and turned bright red. "Might want to get upwind of me for a few minutes."

Katya nodded. "We can finish our talk later."

"That's a good idea. There's probably more where that came from. But thanks. I'll be thinking about what you said."

Up ahead, a different type of conversation was going on.

"Stop calling Sam a pledge and stop cussing so freaking much," Charlie said to Left-Nut. "He's just a kid, and no, he's not going through hell week. And Katya's a nun, goddammit. Let's try to have some class for once. Can you dial it back a little?"

"You mean I can't call you a douche-gargling thundercunt?" Left-Nut asked.

"No."

"How about a fucktard?"

"Nope," Charlie replied.

"A butthead?"

"Reel it back in. Too far," Charlie said.

"A jerkwagon?"

"Acceptable. But in case you haven't noticed, the rest of us are getting along pretty well. Even Vlad has been okay so far. Your shtick is getting old."

Left-Nut dropped his act for just a moment. "I never signed up for this long, sucky adventure, remember? Rob pulled me from the helicopter. I was home free. Heck, I'd already be at the base right this second."

"Oh, I remember. You were willing to leave us behind."

"Not everyone's a hero. You were just like me a few weeks ago. Maybe on the inside you still are."

The words stung Charlie because they were some of the truest Left-Nut had ever spoken. "Look, we're just a few days out from the base. If you're so miserable you can go your own way when we get there. I won't let Rob stop you this time."

As if to signal the end of the discussion, a zombie wearing tattered clothing stumbled onto the trail. Rob instantly ran towards it, prepared to demolish the middle-aged woman with little effort. But Vlad was faster and threw his massive blade after tucking out of an entirely unnecessary monkey-roll. The knife flew past Rob's head and caught the cannibal in the throat, ending the thing's life with a rasp and a gurgle.

"You almost cut my damned nose off!" Rob shouted as he walked briskly towards Vladimir.

The Bulgarian cracked his knuckles and turned to face Rob. "Vlad faster. Always have been. Is why you lost in Vegas."

"That's garbage and you know it. You tapped out and everyone saw it on the video."

Vlad smiled broadly and chuckled. "Is sour grapes."

"Fuck your grapes! Communist bastard."

"Again, not communist, simple fuck."

"Guys, take it down a notch," Charlie said as the twin titans' temperatures rose. Of course, they ignored him.

Left-Nut grinned at Charlie. "One big happy family, huh? Aren't you going to tell them to stop cussing too?"

The shouting brought two more cannibals in from the woods and both of the warriors raced towards them. Vladimir stopped hard before darting to the side and sweeping his leg out for a trip. The zombie fell face first and the fighter was upon it in a flash. He wrapped his arm underneath the creature's chin and broke its neck with a quick snap.

Not to be outdone, Rob tossed his bat aside and grabbed the last zombie underneath both armpits, hoisting the man high into the air until its head got caught between two thick tree limbs. Big Rob jumped up and yanked down hard at the same time. The result was a gruesome pop as the headless body tumbled to the ground with Rob on top of it.

"This is like break dance fighting, but dumber," Smokey said. "And it's gonna get us all killed."

"Enough!" Charlie said with conviction. "Both of you knock it off. And grow up while you're at it."

Rob hung his head while Vlad shrugged his shoulders and retrieved his blade from the downed zombie. The meathead eruption was over, but it could happen again at any time, and Charlie knew it.

Ping and Pong emerged from up ahead to see what all the commotion was about, and Left-Nut spent a few minutes attempting to communicate with them. Finally they agreed to return to their scouting positions, and the long march continued.

Smokey tried to settle things down and struck up a conversation with Vlad. "You were a paratrooper, huh? You'd never catch me jumping out of a plane," Smokey said.

Vlad smiled. "In Bulgaria, sometimes safest option."

"I'd go parachuting if I could," Sam said. "I've never even been in a plane though. I rode the train once."

"First time Vlad jumped, pissed pants. Just like Rob did when—" Screams from nearby stopped him mid-sentence. "Sounds like woman," he said.

A minute later the entire crew was assembled on the edge of the forest with a dilapidated farmhouse dead ahead. Someone was yelling for help from inside and the noise had attracted several cannibals that were now milling about on the porch, attempting to find a way inside.

"Could be a trap. They call out for help and then pick

us all off in the field," Charlie said. "It's an easy way to get supplies."

Sam nodded. "I lost one of my friends kind of like that. We were just looking for food and they shot him. That's why I said we should avoid farmhouses, remember?"

"But who would just be yelling like this in the middle of nowhere?" Smokey said. "Especially if it's gonna draw zombies."

Charlie sighed. That usually meant he would regret the decision that was coming. "How does this sound? We draw those random dickheads over here and take them out. Then we send one volunteer in to check out the situation. We help someone out, and if we find supplies, well that's just the cherry on top. Any takers?" Rob and Vlad both volunteered, and Charlie did not feel like arguing about it. "You'll both go then. After we kill the... hey I said we'd—"

The men were already racing across the field and would arrive at the derelict house any moment.

"I'm going too," Smokey said and took off.

"Fine, all of us then. But spread out," Charlie said and the rest followed him into the open.

The zombies on the porch didn't even notice Vlad until he reached the first one, jabbing his knife through the back of its neck and ripping violently to the side. He turned to face the second but Rob was already swinging away, the pinging sound of his bat marking each death-blow.

As everyone safely reached the porch, Katya said a quick prayer for the fallen while the screams from inside continued. Rob kicked the wooden door off its rusty hinges and it fell inwards, shooting up a cloud of dust while a swarm of flies buzzed around them before disappearing in the wind. The smell inside was as thick and nauseating as the corner store by Charlie's apartment.

Left-Nut backed away. "Nope. I'm not doing it. I'll be waiting out here."

The screaming continued and appeared to be coming from upstairs. "Momma! Momma, get up here now!" Of course, this caused even more zombies to begin running from the woods.

Left-Nut walked inside. "Never mind," he said as the others put the door back into place and shoved a china hutch filled with porcelain pigs up against it.

The rest of the house was a complete disaster, with newspapers, empty cans of double-meat chili, fast food wrappers galore, and plain old junk everywhere.

"Man, this place reminds me of that hoarding show I used to watch," Smokey said as he slipped in a pile of rat droppings. "I'd get baked and think about going into a place like this and just how much fun I'd have recycling everything."

"It was probably already a dump before the shit hit the fan," Left-Nut said as the creatures outside began to pound on the door.

Charlie ignored the chatter. "We should get upstairs and stop that racket."

"I found Momma," Sam said from around a mountain of newspapers in what appeared to be a living room. Nearby, a middle-aged woman sat on a 70s style couch. A shotgun was in the lady's mouth and her brains stained the ceiling as if someone had thrown a large tomato in the air.

"The blood's completely dried up, which means she's been dead several days," Smokey said, playing amateur detective once more. He pointed to the brain matter on the ceiling and did his best David Caruso impersonation. "I guess she was a bit of an... airhead. Yeah!"

Charlie rolled his eyes and then cautiously made his way up a staircase crowded with towers of crumbling books that threatened to tip over at any moment. The yelling intensified as he neared the source. Charlie nodded to the Koreans and then nudged the bedroom door open. Ping and Pong entered, ready to blast away if needed, but they quickly lowered their weapons and walked out, holding their noses.

Charlie peeked around the corner and the stench overwhelmed him. The room smelled even worse than downstairs due to a full-throated bouquet of body odor, human waste, dirty dishes, and a moldy carpet soiled with only god knows what. Sunken into a queen-sized bed was a king-sized man that looked like he weighed nearly five hundred pounds.

He looked at Charlie with a mixture of panic and hope. "Who are you? Where's my Momma!" he asked in a high-pitched whiny voice.

"Shh, shh. It's okay. My names Charlie and—"

"Do you have something for me to eat?" Charlie shook his head and the man went right back to calling for his mother like a baby bird chirping for a worm. An enormous baby bird. "Momma, I'm hungry! Where's my chili! You promised!"

Charlie stepped closer and heard the rotted floor groan underneath him. Left-Nut and Smokey peeked around his shoulder and their combined weight was about to cause a disaster. "Be right back," Charlie said while shoving his friends into the hallway. He took a breath of somewhat fresher air and then gathered everyone downstairs.

"What's going on up there?" Katya asked. "Is someone injured?"

Charlie was about to explain when the screaming upstairs picked up again. After a few seconds it died down, and he was able to get a sentence in. "Let's just say we have a big problem on our hands."

"You think? And here I thought Rob was a fatass," Left-Nut said, earning a punch to the arm. "This guy's a real butterball. We're talking all-you-can-eat zombie buffet."

"Oh, so you're a fat-shamer now too?" Smokey said. "Is there no depth to your depravity?"

"Far from it. I've nailed more fat chicks than anybody. Ain't no shame in my game."

Charlie was about to lose it and none of his usual tricks to ignore Left-Nut were working. "You're like a bad case of herpes. Always flaring up at the worst times."

"Speaking from experience?" Left-Nut turned to smirk at Katya and whispered, "Charlie banged a hooker. Shocking, I know. I was very disappointed in him."

"Just knock it off," Charlie said, trying to calm himself down. "Look, the screamer is his own worst enemy, not ours."

Left-Nut scoffed. "Here we go again with Captain Feelings over here."

"The dude's mom wasn't doing him any favors either, feeding him like that," Smokey said. "Nobody gets that big on their own. You need an accomplice for that."

Charlie nodded. "By the looks of this place the lady was shoveling cans of chili into his mouth and then offed herself when it ran out."

"I will talk with the poor soul," Katya said and headed for the stairs. "Maybe I can calm him down."

Charlie grabbed her wrist. "It isn't safe. The floor's disintegrating as we speak and it could cave in."

"So?" Smokey said. "We can't leave him like this. He'll starve. It might take a while, but still."

"What, you gonna shoot him?" Left-Nut asked. "Kind of goes against this humanitarian streak you guys have going."

As the argument continued, Sam got bored and went off to explore the rest of the house. He returned moments later with an ashen look on his face. "There's another body over there."

"And?" Left-Nut said.

"You might want to take a look. This one's different."

Indeed it was. Inside the dining room was the dead man in question, propped up at the table and wearing a homemade Christmas sweater. Of course, Smokey's

141

amateur sleuthing skills kicked into high gear as he weighed the situation. "This place is giving me the creeps now. Homeboy has been dead for years."

"I'll bite," Charlie said. "How would you know?"

"Basic forensics. This is more of a mummy than a corpse. The body doesn't smell too awful and the skin is drawn back." Smokey pointed to the eyes. "And those have been sewn shut like you might see on an old shrunken head. It makes my skin crawl just thinking about it."

"So they just kept a dead body in the house like it's no big deal?" Sam said. "I'm freaked out too. Can we go?"

Left-Nut began to chuckle, though the sentiment behind it was obviously fake. "Bravo, Charlie. You've led us into the Manson family's summer home. We've got a suicide Granny, King Tut over here, zombies on the porch, and Fatty McFatfuck upstairs screaming like god-damned porn star."

The pitiful wails picked up again, even louder this time. Then they stopped mid-scream. Charlie looked around the room and noticed somebody was missing.

"Where's Vlad?"

Nobody answered.

A creaking noise revealed the answer as the Bulgarian came down the cluttered stairs with a blank look on his face. "Is done," he said matter-of-factly and wiped his blade on a dirty towel hanging from the banister.

"What is done?" Charlie asked pointedly.

"Severed artery and big boy bled out in seconds. Not painful."

Charlie blinked rapidly. "Damn, Vlad, that's just not right. We could have done something else."

"Right, wrong? It no matter, is done. Besides, you want rescue pregnant girlfriend or waste time babysitting Porky Pig?"

Left-Nut nodded in agreement. "He has you there, Chuck."

Furious, Charlie measured his words carefully as Rob stood by his side, itching for a violent reckoning years in the making. "Regardless, you just joined our crew and you're already—"

"No, you joined Vlad's crew," the fighter said with hard eyes and a cold demeanor. Charlie stared right back and it appeared a bloodletting was imminent.

Then Vlad winked. "Just kidding. Come on, we kill guys on porch and get moving. Lots of ground to cover."

The tension in the room dropped, but Charlie was left wondering about the newest member of their group. Was Vlad testing him? Was he a calculating manipulator, a madman, or just an idiot? The Bulgarian grinned as he opened the door to eviscerate the zombies outside and it became quite clear. He was all of the above. And he was a big fucking problem.

Chapter 17
Old Baggage

Xavier dragged Mary in circles through the forest for several hours and ended up somewhat close to where they had started, next to the highway of smashed up zombies. He had correctly guessed that his victims would flee the area, and he now wanted to find a vehicle to do the same.

He'd also used the last of his ammo on some random cannibals and now held his captive through the threat of violence alone. With mild-mannered Mary, it was more than enough to keep her in check.

Unfortunately for Xavier none of the cars were usable, so he had to figure out what to do next. The last of the Gutter Punks decided to rest for a bit while pondering the situation. Free time for a sadist is always dangerous to those under their control, and Mary would find this out in short order.

Xavier used a cracked shard of windshield glass to cut out a seatbelt, which he used to fashion hand restraints and a blindfold for his captive.

"Don't worry about me running away," Mary said, speaking the first words to him since the whole fiasco started. "I have nowhere to go since you took me away from my friends. I wouldn't last five minutes out there."

Xavier chuckled in an unseemly manner. "If they were your friends they wouldn't have left you. Anyways, those aren't supposed to keep you from running away. I have something... different in mind."

Before she had time to realize what that may be, the cretin lurched forward and shoved his tongue forcefully down Mary's throat. She froze up, earning a swat to the ear. "What are you doing?" she asked and pulled her head back.

Again, the chuckling. "This is called foreplay. Do you know what that is?"

"Not really."

Xavier sighed. "You're taking all the fun out of this." He scanned the road around them for any dangers and turned back. "All right, you're gonna dance for me. And make it sexy. I don't have all day."

"But—"

"Just fucking do it!"

Mary swayed around in a shambling manner, looking more confused and disoriented than anything else. She thought about shaking the blindfold loose and making a break for the woods, but with her hands tied it would be near impossible to escape. She realized this was how Jen must have felt and then began to sob, thinking about the death of her friend.

"I said *sexy*, bitch. Did you fall off the turnip truck or something?" Xavier set down his empty pistol, adjusted the ratty bowler hat he'd taken from a corpse, and clenched his fists. The woman was merely slowing him down and she wouldn't be around for much longer because of it. But she could still serve his nefarious purposes in one way or another.

He opened the back door to a broken down SUV and shoved Mary inside headfirst, causing her to crash into the door on the opposite side.

"I've been around a lot of women in my day. Sluts, crack heads, soccer moms looking for a quick fix before driving back to the suburbs. You don't fit any of those groups at all. If I had to guess, I'd say you're a virgin. That true?" Mary didn't answer, and Xavier kept right on talking. "They say your first time is the one that you always remember. They say it should be special. But I gotta be honest, it's not gonna be."

The chuckling ended as he approached the open door with a stern face. "My first time was with my third grade teacher, Mr. Murphy. Kind of hard to forget that, though I tried."

Mary grasped for straws. "I'm sorry, but hurting me won't—"

"Shut it. This is gonna happen, so you'd better just accept it. And you'll want to stay quiet, because if any of these creatures comes around you're my escape plan. Capiche?"

Mary had no clue what "capiche" meant, but she understood the rest of his rant quite well. So she closed her eyes and hoped against hope that there was someone nearby with a noble heart and a heroic streak. Some kind person that could end the madness.

Of course, there wasn't. But Xavier gagged and then slumped over dead all the same. The glass shard he had used to threaten Mary now protruded from the man's throat and blood spurted into the car, quickly pooling on the floor amongst a pile of spilled french fries and a half-eaten pouch of Big League Chew.

Marquell Washington shoved the body aside and pulled Mary out by her feet. Then he retrieved the pouch of gum and put the rest in his mouth. Happily, it was grape – his favorite flavor.

Like Xavier, Marquell had made some assumptions, and had been proven correct. Primarily he had guessed that Xavier would return to the area and would let his guard down in favor of more immediate urges. It was elementary for Marquell in some regards. After all, the gang virtuoso had used his Doctorate-level comprehension of the criminal mind to rule the streets, and ultimately the very prison he had ended up in.

Marquell untied Mary and then took Xavier's hat, placing it upon his own mound of matted dreadlocks in a symbolic act of victory. Years earlier, Marquell had successfully sued the Illinois Department of Corrections

146

for the right to keep those very locks under a religious exemption to the department's grooming regulations. It had been a test case for Marquell and a chance to get his toes wet in the world of lawfare.

He had several more pending cases, but they'd been interrupted by the zombie outbreak. Not that it mattered. Marquell had found his freedom regardless of legal status. But it was that freedom which now smacked him square in the face as he and Mary stared at each other in the darkness, crickets chirping loudly and mosquitoes buzzing around them. Marquell had never left Chicago, much less ventured to the countryside, and he was totally out of his element. It didn't help that *The Blair Witch Project* kept popping up in his mind.

The two quietly walked along the road for a few minutes before Mary mustered the courage to speak. "Not that I'm complaining, but why did you come for me?"

"Russ said I'd be harder to see in the dark. I guess the moron was right for once," Marquell said with his infectious grin. The truth of the matter was he had no idea why he volunteered to rescue her, just that he hadn't hesitated. Maybe he wanted to wear a white hat for once. Or possibly, like Trent, he was searching for some piece of atonement for his past misdeeds. There were plenty of them to choose from.

"You didn't say why, though."

"Don't know," Marquell answered honestly.

She accepted the answer and moved on. "What about the other women?"

"They went to find help for the guy that got shot. Trent, my... associate." Marquell dared not call him a friend, although he had grown to respect him in some measure over the past few days. "The brunette girl didn't make it. Sorry."

"Yeah, I saw. She was a great friend." Mary changed the subject to avoid breaking down. "Are they coming back to get us?"

Marquell stopped walking. "I'm not sure. They said they would." The doubt in Marquell's answer was obvious. He had no real expectation the others would come for them as promised, and he was seriously questioning the decision that put him in the current predicament.

It was his turn to change the subject. "My name's Marquell, by the way." The hardened criminal was trying his best to talk in a manner he pictured as "civilized," but it came off more like he was nervous. And with the unfamiliar noises of the nearby forest calling out, he was.

"Mary."

"That was my Mom's name," Marquell said and stopped walking.

"Oh, that's—"

"I killed her."

Mary apprehensively sucked air in through her teeth. "Umm, okay." She always had a knack for creating awkward conversations, but this one took the cake. Why two men in a row had decided to tell her their childhood secrets was also a mystery.

"I killed her," Marquell repeated, much quieter this time. Then he collapsed in a heap, sobbing uncontrollably like he never had before. So many emotions, so much baggage, with only one direction for it all to come out. He couldn't stop, and Mary, never one for profound conversations, was thrown for a loop. So she did what came naturally, and got down in the dirt with her new friend, holding the sobbing man close.

Comforted by the gesture, Marquell launched into a laundry list of horrible details from his life. There were the people he killed, the people he tortured, the ones whose lives he had ruined both before and after the apocalypse, and those he had just plain shit on. Drug dealers, foster families, social workers, and random strangers had all felt his wrath in one form or another. Tale after gruesome tale drove this point home in explicit detail.

Mary soaked it all in while trying to formulate a response. It took her a while, but that was okay, because Marquell had plenty to tell.

"Maybe you had no choice? I mean, would you have done any of that stuff if you grew up in Naperville with a mom named Tiffany and a dad that worked at the power plant?"

Marquell shrugged. "I don't know, but I doubt it. You're talking the motherfuckin' classical nature versus nurture argument? I have pondered that shit before. Believe me."

"I have no clue what that means, but I doubt it too," Mary said. "There's a nice person inside you, or else you wouldn't have come to save me. That took guts, and heart. You risked your life for a nobody."

"No, you're a somebody." Marquell wiped the last tear from his eye and stood up. "You've made it a lot farther than millions of other people in our situation. Soldiers, politicians, scientists... they're all dead, but you made it."

"So have you."

Marquell nodded and sniffled one final time. He no longer questioned his decision. "Let's go. Maybe they'll pick us up. If not, we'll find someplace safe for when the sun comes up. Can't risk being tired and out in the open." He helped her up and then turned to walk off. "And don't tell anyone about my little breakdown here or I'll have to kill you."

He was joking. Sort of. But after hearing some of the things Marquell was capable of, Mary had already decided to stay firmly on his tiny good side. She wasn't so dumb after all.

He swatted at a mosquito. "Motherfuckin' bugs. I mean, damned bugs. Trent was right, I need to stop saying that so much. My vocabulary, my demeanor, I think a lot of it's just been a costume of sorts to survive. To play the part, you look the part. Can't be soft behind bars, you know? But I've been wearing it so long I don't

149

know where the costume ends and the real me begins. I'm almost scared to find out."

Marquell's continuing insights were deep and travelled far above Mary's head for the most part. But she smiled and nodded in agreement just the same. She was beginning to like him very much, warts and all.

Maybe it was a rebirth of sorts, or the stress of his screwed-up life in general, or the fact that he had finally made himself vulnerable for once, but something downright electric was jolting through Marquell's body. And it was glorious. He breathed in the country air, truly taking it in for once, and exhaled. The tight muscles in his powerful shoulders relaxed slightly as the weight of several lifetimes blew away in the night air.

Headlights appeared in the distance, and the two ducked behind the nearest car as a precaution. A semi approached at high speed, and its unique paint job was hard not to recognize. So Marquell and Mary stepped into the road while the truck came to a loud stop, its driver having applied the Jake brake with abandon.

The doors swung open and Russ hopped out casually while the women ran to their friend. "Nice hat, you big pimp," he said with a wink. "Don't look so surprised, bro. I said we'd come back for you."

Jackie and Padma showered Mary with hugs and then Jackie hustled her into the cab before any more unexpected problems could arise.

Marquell adjusted his new cap. "Not my typical style, but it's pretty dope. And the previous owner won't be needing it anymore." He looked at Padma. "Did you find what you were looking for?"

She nodded. "It was amazing. Russ just walked in and got the stuff. The cannibals ignored him completely. Even better, I had Trent stabilized a few hours later."

"I told you, I'm like a zombie Chuck Norris," Russ said with a grin that made him look somewhat insane. "Or a redneck samurai. Yeah, I like that better."

"You mean dead-neck," Padma said, barely containing a smile. She was actually enjoying her verbal sparring with Russ on a limited scale, but unfortunately her opportunity to do so was decidedly unlimited.

Russ tilted his head at the attractive doctor. "She wants the D. I know it."

"Is Trent gonna make it, then?" Marquell asked, somehow unable to hide the fact that he was starting to care. Why? He hadn't figured that out yet. The cop had been a pain in his ass the past few days, was obviously a racist, and had very few redeeming qualities. Then again, Marquell wasn't much of a peach either.

"It's touch and go," Padma said. "He has a chance since I stopped the bleeding and removed both bullets. But if an infection sets in..."

Drawn by Russ's gratuitously loud braking, zombies began wandering in from every surrounding area, and it became necessary to head out in a hurry. Marquell climbed inside the crowded semi as Russ pulled away, leaving the trail of ravenous monsters in his wake.

The hillbilly cracked open a freshly looted but rather expired beer and tossed one to his new partner in crime. "Trent's in the back resting, so we're gonna have to decide where to go without him. We have about sixty miles of fuel, give or take."

"Will it be enough to reach that airport I told you about?" Marquell asked and took a drink. The beer was skunky and warm as piss, but after the past few days it was much appreciated.

"I was kinda wantin' to go fishing, but your idea's probably better. Let's go with that."

"Punch it then," Marquell said and took another drink. Then he tipped forward and snored loudly as he fell asleep in an instant, spilling his beer.

Russ leaned over and grabbed the can, nearly driving off the road before finishing it himself. "Party foul, alcohol abuse."

Chapter 18
Oasis

Food poisoning. It's a pretty common occurrence in most apocalyptic scenarios, whether it be in the aftermath of a meteor strike, financial ruin, sex-bot uprising or, in this case, a dreaded zombie and military invasion combo. Food poisoning is also just as likely to kill you as anything else in the heretofore-mentioned catastrophe.

Charlie was finding this out the hard way as he struggled to keep pace while becoming more dehydrated by the minute. Sam had told him not to eat apples off the ground, but Rob had convinced him otherwise. Of course, the big guy seemed just fine while Charlie wanted to die. "Man, I need some water. And thank God we brought toilet paper," he said while holding his stomach.

"Eat one of those spiky plants over there, it's what they call a succulent and should quench your thirst," Smokey replied, once again trying to prove how in touch with nature he was.

"Succulent? Wasn't that your nickname in high school?"

Charlie's eyes flashed daggers at him. "Shut it, Left-Nut." His head was pounding and he was in no mood for Left-Nut's mouth. He went over and began to chew on the aloe vera-looking plant. It was bitter and slimy, but it would do until they found a stream. "And we have to ration our water better next time," Charlie said while choking the plant down. "We went through our supply way too fast. Rob, I'm looking mostly in your direction."

"No fair. I'm a big boy, I gotta drink a lot."

"At least on this old country road we're making some good time now," Smokey said. "With the Koreans scouting ahead we're bound to find water soon." Following the gravel road west from the Maniac house had been a solid decision so far, and they had covered more ground in the past few hours than the rest of the day combined. At this rate, so long as no Chinese patrols were in the area, they would reach Cantonville in several days. If Charlie could stop pooping every five minutes.

Pong, the younger of the Koreans, came walking back towards the group in an excited state. After Left-Nut bungled the translation horribly, Pong was able to convince everyone to hurry their pace by using hand gestures and high-pitched noises.

Soon the road took them around a bend in the forest where they caught up with Ping, now doing recon while hiding in some bushes. Ahead they saw a large compound surrounded by recreational vehicles with a fading billboard out front.

Sam read the sign aloud: "Crazy Pat's R.V. World. Prices so low, they're crazy."

Ping crawled out from his spot and held up two fingers, then made a walking motion with them.

Charlie was still not thinking clearly because of his condition, and was starting to get reckless. "Okay, so there's just two people here. I think. We might as well introduce ourselves with the numbers we have. We need water, better directions, and if we could get one of those R.V.s... well, that would be tits."

"Not good idea," Vlad said. "No element of surprise."

"I don't give a shit," Charlie said. He pointed to the Koreans. "They still have some bullets left and can keep us covered."

"Not coming with to get shot. Good luck," Vlad said and found a nice spot in the shade. "How you say, amateur hour?"

Charlie shrugged. "Katya and Sam, stay in the back and everybody fan out. Don't provoke these guys, but don't take any shit either. They have more than enough to share the wealth."

Ready for bear, they marched through a small gap in the cyclone barbed wire, then spread out with Charlie in the lead as he walked towards a run-down trailer. A man and a woman sat outside on a wooden deck, enjoying the mild weather with some iced tea and carrot cake.

"Hello there," Charlie said as he approached with his arms up in a gesture of peace. "Lovely day we're having," he added while his stomach gurgled and took a turn for the worse. Charlie stopped walking and gritted his teeth momentarily until the pain passed. It did, but he was liable to shit his pants at any moment, and that would do little to help him negotiate.

"Sure is. But I bet you're not here to pontificate about the weather though, now are you?" The mobile home salesman was in his mid-fifties with a silver comb-over and a beer belly. He was sharp, straight to the point, and keen on making a sale. Which wasn't going to happen.

"No, sir," Charlie said. "Not exactly."

"I take it you're here to shop for mobile homes then? That's good. That's real good, because I've got a lot of top-end models here at rock-bottom prices. They don't call me Crazy—"

"How rock bottom are we talking?" Charlie asked and grimaced as the knot in his gut twisted again.

Crazy Pat's demeanor went south in a hurry as he looked to his female companion. "Hell, I think we got some more freeloaders here." He looked back to Charlie as the others in the group slowly drew closer. "I'll make this nice and simple. If you got fifty thousand dollars cash money, we can do business. Can't let you take one of my babies off the lot for less than that. As you can guess, these aren't exactly being produced anymore."

"That's horse—"

"It is the supreme law of the business jungle, supply and demand," Pat said, rather pleased with himself. "You have to pay to play my friend."

Charlie looked closer at the man's wheelchair-bound companion, and it became apparent that the term "crazy" on the sign was a rare bit of truth in advertising. The woman was covered in makeup, flawlessly gorgeous, and entirely made of synthetic materials. She was a high-priced sex doll.

Of course, Left-Nut noticed this as well and came up right next to Charlie in a hurry. "Hot damn, you got yourself the Maserati of bang dolls right there. Is that an x-class or are my eyes deceiving me?"

Crazy Pat was plainly agitated. "Now you watch your smart mouth. Cassandra is a classy lady, and I won't have you disparaging her."

"Shut it," Charlie said to Left-Nut and then addressed Pat once more. "Look, while we chat, is there any fresh water we could fill up with? We haven't come across any in a while and we're awful thirsty. We do have women and children with us." His stomach gurgled so loudly that Pat could hear it all the way on the porch.

"No freebies around here. There's a lake about two miles down the road." He looked to the doll. "What's that, sweetheart?" Then he nodded at Left-Nut. "She doesn't like the way Whitey there's looking at her. So I'm gonna ask you to kindly leave. Unless we can do some business after all?"

For whatever reason Left-Nut was feeling bold, and stepped towards the salesman. "How about we just take one of those shiny new R.V.s with us?" Licking his lips, Left-Nut didn't take his eyes off the doll as he continued, "Even better, why don't I take little Cassandra there on a trip to pound town?" He winked at the doll. "What do you think about that, classy lady? Up for a ride on the baloney pony?" It might have been the first time a doll had been threatened during the commission of an attempted armed robbery. Thankfully, those types of statistics were no longer kept in post-governmental America.

Pat calmly whispered something to his pseudo-girlfriend, raised a pistol he had concealed behind his table, and cocked the hammer back. "Make a move and Powder there dies first. Feeling froggy?"

Charlie was about to intervene in the tense standoff, but then shut his mouth as a light bulb went off. Could this be it? The moment Left-Nut had finally mouthed off to the wrong person? The moment he would die a painful death because of said mouth running? Charlie held his breath – and his stomach – and hoped so.

Cautiously, Vladimir opened the front door of the mobile home from inside and emerged directly behind Crazy Pat. He held his knife to the man's throat. "Negotiations have taken turn in our favor, yes?"

But Pat played it cool. "Not from my perspective. You could kill me, but that won't get you want you want. No, nothing but fifty thousand dollars will do that." He whispered again to his doll, "Close your eyes honey, I don't want you to see this."

Vlad laughed. "I guess we find out."

"You see, first you'll have to find the keys I've buried in the forest. Then you'll have to find one of the batteries hidden in a different spot. After that, you'll need to travel twenty miles to town just to haul some fuel back."

Vlad removed the knife from the man's throat and Crazy Pat nodded. "Glad you came to your... hey what are you doing?" Vlad had stepped away from Pat only to put the knife against the doll's supple neck instead.

"Negotiations open once more," Vlad said dryly.

Once calm and collected, Crazy Pat was now about to crack. The love of his life, albeit a weird and non-reciprocating one, faced certain decapitation and possibly worse if Left-Nut had his way.

Charlie watched and waited, ready to give the signal for his Korean allies to shoot. If it happened to come after

156

a certain somebody got gunned down, well, all the better. But Katya ruined his plan in an instant, stepping in front of Left-Nut and entering the line of fire. "This is getting out of control and we are better than this. No one has to get hurt."

Vlad tilted his head in confusion and pulled the knife away slightly. They were close to obtaining desperately needed transportation, by hook or crook, and the nun was about to ruin it. He put the knife back. "She doesn't speak for me. Keys, battery, gas. Where are they?"

Charlie shook off his selfish haze and came to his senses. "She's right, Vlad. We are better than this. Put the knife down and we'll be on our way."

Vlad's arm trembled in anger for a few long moments and then he backed away in disgust. The disturbing and ridiculous confrontation was over. After a few choice parting words, the gang retreated from the compound and went on their way down the gravel road while battling sore feet, fatigue, thirst and anger.

Nobody spoke for a few minutes until Smokey broke the ice. "That guy needs a checkup from the neck up. Crazy douche."

"I'd like to take a crack at his girlfriend though," Left-Nut said and looked off into space, undoubtedly forming some sort of lurid fantasy in his depraved mind. "She was a cutie. Nice boobs. Firm pooper."

"Would you stop talking about that damned blow-up doll?" Smokey said.

"It's not a blow-up doll, it's a finely handcrafted work of art. That you put your dick in."

Charlie halted in his tracks. "You know, Left-Nut and Vlad, we better get on the same page about..." he stopped midsentence, closing his eyes. "And I just shit my pants."

*   *   *

The lake was right where the crazy bastard had said it would be and the group reached it within an hour. But the water didn't look anywhere near potable. It was covered with moss and algae and had a definite green tint to it.

"Lots of critters in that soup," Rob said. "I wouldn't drink it."

"No problem. We just start a small fire and boil it first," Sam said, eager to add his Boy Scout skills to the mix. "Katya, can we use your pot?"

"Yes," she answered clearly. It was amazing how quickly her voice was coming back, literally and figuratively.

As they neared the water's edge, Vlad and Smokey went to investigate an abandoned van parked nearby. From their reactions they had found something of note.

"Gross as it is, I gotta get cleaned up," Charlie said and headed for the water. "Katya, if you could get that going, I'd appreciate it."

"Of course," she said and took the kindling Sam had gathered. Soon she had a small fire roaring and was eager to bring the discolored water to a boil. Like Sam, proving her usefulness was a high priority.

Smokey and Vlad joined the others by the lake to show off their discovery while Sam jumped into the murky water and swam out, like any boy his age would do in a similar circumstance.

Charlie was enjoying his swim as well. The thick water was warm and actually very soothing on his many bumps and bruises. After walking a while in soiled underwear, the value of getting clean could not be overstated.

Smokey held out his hand. "Check it. Somebody's picnic got interrupted and they left a few joints and sandwiches behind."

"And vodka," Vlad added happily before tipping a clear bottle back.

"The sandwiches were trash, of course, but these bad

boys look just fine." Smokey lit one up and took the first toke, hard. As in, almost the whole thing.

Left-Nut grabbed it next and took a much smaller hit, coughing loudly. He turned to one of the Koreans standing guard nearby. "Hey, Donger, you want a hit?"

Smokey frowned. "You mean Pong?"

"That's not his real name either," Left-Nut said.

Rob took the joint without asking and finished it off with relish. Then he turned philosophical. "I'm enjoying this for sure, but I do wonder what happened to whoever left it behind. I mean, did they get eaten by zombies or the slime monster from *Creepshow Two*?" He shivered while pointing to the water that Charlie and Sam were swimming in. "That movie gave me nightmares for months. No way I'd go in that nastiness."

"Feels pretty good to me," Charlie said. "A little slimy, but overall not bad."

Vlad set the cheap handle of vodka down. "Enjoying your soak, eh? Would be better to be driving to destination."

"Just drop it," Charlie said.

But he wouldn't drop it. "Should have killed that man and taken recreational vehicle. Could have been to base in less than one hour."

Smokey shook his head. "We aren't killers. And you heard the guy, how could we have gotten the vehicles moving?"

"Was bluffing. Is why Charlie not good leader like Vlad. You hesitate, you die. So does everyone depending on you. Act on instincts and survive."

Charlie gritted his teeth, fighting the strain of dehydration and his annoyance at what was becoming a recurring issue. Katya couldn't finish boiling the water soon enough. "Listen, stop jamming me up, comrade."

"Again, not Russian. Besides, if Vlad jamming you up, Vlad jam you up so bad you have no room for peanut butter on your toast."

"I think we're talking about different things, buddy." Charlie turned to his friends. "It's like Vidu all over again."

"No idea what that means," the Bulgarian said. "Anyways... must go leave shit in woods. Vlad prairie-dogging." He walked away.

"God, that guy's a dildo," Charlie said quietly.

Rob nodded. "Yup. It was your idea to bring him along though, remember? I'm the guy that wanted to beat his ass."

"I still think he can help us," Charlie said as he waded to shore. "But if he keeps challenging me on every single thing, then—"

"Ow," Sam said loudly. "Ow!" he screamed a moment later, as he was pulled partially underwater.

Charlie dove back into the murky drink as Sam flailed about in a panic, screaming that something was biting his foot. After swimming the twenty yards to reach him, Charlie grabbed the kid's arms and pulled him towards the beach. As they reached the edge of the water it became evident what had attacked him since the creature was still firmly attached.

"Snapping turtle!" Smokey exclaimed.

Sam tried kicking it loose, but it wouldn't budge. "Get it off, get it off!"

Butt naked, Charlie grabbed a large rock and bashed the reptile's head several times until it released its powerful grip. A few more knocks and the ugly beast was dead.

Sam writhed in pain. His foot was pretty chewed up, but he still had all his toes. "Ow. I must have stepped on it."

"I thought a zombie had you there for a second," Charlie said, then realized he was standing naked in front of everyone. He covered himself with a shirt and looked to Katya with a smile. "Keep that water boiling because it looks like we're gonna have turtle soup for dinner."

"Wow, that thing must weigh fifty pounds," Smokey said as the Koreans came in with smiles, also excited to have meat on the menu for a change.

"Yeah, it was a nasty sucker. I'm glad I found that rock right away. I'm surprised Rob hadn't already bashed its..." Charlie looked around. "Hey, where is Rob?"

The jovial giant had disappeared during the chaos. "I thought he went in the water to help Sam," Smokey said and shrugged.

That's when Charlie's eyes got big. "The dumbass can't swim!"

"Oh, fuck," Smokey said as they all jumped into the lake in a hurry.

Charlie took the lead. "Everyone form a line and spread out, he can't be that far in."

A minute or two passed and there was no sign of him as Rob's friends frantically scoured the waters. And then Ping raised his hand while shouting something unintelligible. Sure enough, they pulled Big Rob to the surface and then dragged him ashore with great effort.

He was pale, his big lungs were full of water, and the rest of him was empty of life. Charlie tried in vain to administer CPR, but simply didn't know what he was doing. Frustrated, he lashed out at Sam. "Dammit, why did you get in the water anyways?"

"I just wanted to go swimming, like old times," he said and hid his face.

Katya clutched the crying child to her chest. "Now's not the time!"

Charlie ignored her and tried mouth to mouth again before doing some half-assed chest compressions. The others stood around in shock. Nothing worked. Precious time passed and it became painfully clear. Viking Rob Magnusson, the man, the myth, was gone.

Chapter 19
Prison Break

Aedes albopictus, also known as the Asian tiger mosquito due to its distinctive striped pattern, had been an invasive species in Illinois for decades. In normal times the tiny creatures were plentiful, impossible to eradicate, and sometimes deadly. Now with legions of zombies to feed upon and countless pools of untreated water, the pest had become a plague of biblical scope. Sharpshooter Gus smacked one on his forehead a little too late, and then wiped the blood off his hand. "Gotcha," he said and itched at the growing welt.

The prison guard had continued manning the observation tower after the apocalypse much as he had before it, with shoot to kill orders and a hard-on to carry out those orders. But he had become a bit more vigilant since the night of Marquell's escape. Gus claimed a pack of zombies had finished the gang leader off, and since nobody was able to prove otherwise, that was that.

A cloud moved ever so slightly from its position blocking the moon, and Gus discovered that another invasive species, also from Asia, had come out that night. Only this one was even deadlier than the first. Nearby, Chinese troops began massing behind piles of rubble and battle-worn tanks. Even worse, through his high-powered binoculars, Gus could see mobile artillery rolling into place.

It was time to get to work. The sharpshooter put half a tin of Redman chew into his mouth and set his AR-15 into firing position. Then he hit the buzzer and alerted the entire prison of the impending attack. They had known it was coming for days, and the prison occupants had prepared as best they could. But after seeing the forces arrayed against them, Gus already knew what the outcome would be. He put his headphones on, turned Garth Brooks up, and began blasting Chinese soldiers from five hundred yards.

Inside the prison was a flurry of activity as the guards and their families took up fighting positions and dug in. Like the Alamo, all parties realized there would be no quarter given. Unlike the Alamo, where the defense was led by the likes of Davey Crockett and Jim Bowie, a gorgeous socialite with steel nerves and a rock-hard body commanded the prison garrison.

Heather McCabe took to the intercom as mortars landed like tiny meteors all around the compound, blasting away at the structures and killing inhabitants by the handful. "Now is the time we've prepared for," she said quietly, then cleared her throat before speaking in a more authoritative manner. "We're ready. We survived the plague, we survived the riots, and we'll survive this. It's time to teach them a lesson they'll never forget. This is our prison, and more importantly, this is our country! Now fight with all you have, and know I'll be right here fighting with you."

A raucous cheer went up in all corners of Richard Daley Prison while two Chinese tanks rolled towards the outer fence, with scores of People's Liberation Army Marines trailing behind. Heather rose from her office chair and sprinted into the hallway as more explosions went off and the lights flickered ominously. She could hear the tanks moving closer even from deep inside the complex. Time was short.

Meanwhile, Gus's targets were moving steadily closer to him and he was now able to potshot the soldiers much more rapidly. However, the pair of tanks had closed to within two hundred yards and would breach the perimeter within minutes. Then it would be game over. Not only that, but the explosive rounds were getting closer to the tower as the mortar teams zeroed in on his position.

Gus stopped firing, spit, and grabbed his walkie-talkie. "Release the hounds," he said, and then landed a spurting head shot on a crouching soldier.

Another alarm sounded and the outer gates swung open. In an instant, hundreds of hungry cannibals that had been trapped between the outer and inner fences streamed towards the advancing Chinese. Most of them were immediately cut down by small arms fire, but a dozen plowed into the ranks of the attackers, creating a temporary moment of mayhem.

But the zombies were just a distraction.

BOOOOM!

A disabled tractor-trailer stuffed with fertilizer and thousands of ball bearings blew up next to the tanks. The force of the mega-explosion sent body parts flying, knocked the treads off both tanks, and shook the entire prison.

Iraq War veterans can come in handy if one ever needs to make I.E.Ds. Luckily the prison had several on staff that could take the homemade explosives apart and put them back together in their sleep. The Chinese military had failed to anticipate this capability, and their cannon fodder paid for it dearly.

Next, several dozen defenders emerged from a safe house a block away in a surprise counter-offensive, making their way towards the self-propelled 155 mm howitzers parked half a mile away. If those bad boys went live, it would be all over but the crying.

"Nice," Gus said when he saw his own guys working quietly towards the target. Then he got back to his own task at hand as stray bullets raked the tower from several directions. More Garth Brooks, more killing.

While the fighting picked up, Heather grabbed her beloved dog along with two heavy bags and began

164

making her way through the prison in a hurry. She passed crying women and children along the way, and paused just long enough to tell them what they wanted to hear. Sadly, it was all bullshit.

Heather opened a final door and walked outside to where a bright yellow Bell 204 helicopter was waiting for her on the basketball courts, gassed up, blades spinning, and ready for takeoff.

The pilot named Jake, a grizzled vet, hopped out and tossed the dog inside before helping her with the luggage. He wasn't happy, and shouted above the sound of the blades to let her know just that. "I told you we were already close to our weight limit, now you show up with all this shit?"

The recreation building behind them burst into flames and the windows shattered, sending glass flying all about. "I don't think we should be arguing about this right now!" Heather shouted back.

"Do you want to crash two miles out because the damned helicopter is off balance? Pick one and toss the other."

"Fine," she said and chucked a large green duffel bag to the ground. It clanged loudly and stopped right in place.

As the two finished their bickering over maximum gross weight capacity, a garbage truck crashed through both outer fences and Chinese soldiers swiftly followed through the opening, demonstrating that they had some tricks of their own. Guards shot at them from the rooftops, but the sprinting soldiers quickly spread out and found hiding spots. Soon they were mounting effective counter fire and dropping the guards one by one.

They pressed their advance, then noticed the smell of gasoline too late. The overgrown and parched grass ignited with the help of a Molotov cocktail, and many of the Chinese marines suffered horrible burns. But the flames died down soon enough and more troops kept pouring in.

By this time Gus had already retreated to a rooftop farther back and continued to tear up the opposition with blistering and accurate shooting. When the helicopter rose up behind him and he was momentarily face to face with Heather, Gus was equal parts surprised and pissed. And so he did what any self-respecting merchant of death would do in a similar situation: he lit that sucker up.

Jake was forced to pull back hard as AR-15 rounds peppered the windshield and effortlessly zipped through the back of the helicopter. The dog barked wildly as tracer fire followed close behind while they sped off, and it became clear both sides were shooting at them in earnest.

Gus watched the chopper disappear into the night and swatted another mosquito as it landed on his nose. "Gotcha." Then an artillery shell exploded on top of the roof and the talented sharpshooter was instantly oblite-rated, leaving behind nothing more than a stain and a funky smell. The thunder rolled as the firing continued.

Initially the Chinese command had sought to use the prison as headquarters and didn't want it destroyed. But when their artillery was threatened by a surprise coun-terattack from tactical shotgun-wielding prison guards, the decision was made to light the place up. And so they ground it to dust with barrage after barrage, knowing that each explosion would draw more of the infected to the area. But the zombies were incapable of strategy and trickery, and so were much more easily dealt with.

Heather saw the heavy blasts in the prison and knew right away that the battle was over. So she turned around and focused on the empty black sky in front of her, strik-ing the faces of those left behind from her thoughts. In their hour of need, she had left them to die. But above all, Heather was a survivor, and she just didn't give a damn.

"What was in the bag you threw out, anyways?" Jake asked as he adjusted several instruments on the panel.

"You don't want to know," she said flatly. "Trust me."

"Well, now you have to tell me," the pilot pressed.

"Gold. Lots and lots of gold."

"And the one you kept?" Jake asked, his thick eyebrows furrowed in amazement.

"Dog food."

Chapter 20
Graveyard

Charlie put his clothes on and joined the others as they stood around on the beach. The only noise anyone could hear was the sound of weeping and the infrequent waves lapping at the sand.

That was, until Vlad emerged from the woods with a quizzical look on his face. "What all that commotion? You trying to get zombie rave going?"

Katya pointed to Rob's motionless body. "There was an accident."

"Oh, fuck Vlad's life. Can't even drop log in woods without major calamity."

"He didn't even scream for help or anything. He just... disappeared," Smokey said amidst tears.

Vlad shoved Smokey aside and dropped to the ground next to his old adversary. "This not way for warrior to die." He placed his hands on Rob's barrel chest, pushing forcefully and with speed as if he were beating him up in the process. "Come on, big chicken." Pump, pump, pump. "Come on, big chicken!" Pump, pump, pump. He slapped Rob's lifeless face multiple times. "COME ON BIG CHICKEN!"

Rob had been going towards the glowing light and the smell of baby back ribs for what seemed like an hour. He could unmistakably hear Vidu talking about scuba diving with Abraham Lincoln and Blake whining about his retirement fund going unspent. Just a few more steps and he'd be on the other side. Was that a bucket of hot wings and a pitcher of Pale Horse Ale glistening in the sun?

Vlad punched his old adversary in the gut and Big Rob spit out a massive lungful of water before grabbing Vlad's throat and choking him with the strength of a panicking beast, letting out a roar.

Vladimir struggled to break the man's iron grip, but still cracked a smile. "Little help, please," he managed to mumble and everyone grabbed at Rob's arms, prying them away with great effort.

Rob rolled over and puked up more of the greenish water while Vlad massaged a purple throat and spit on the ground several times. "Breath smells like depressed dog's butthole." Rob puked again and Vlad continued, "Anyways, welcome back to land of living. Choke me again, and you're headed right back the other way."

"Fuck you," Rob said between gasps of air. "And thanks."

"How the hell did you do that?" Charlie asked, impressed for once with the newest member of their group. "I thought he was dead for sure."

"We have lot of drownings in Bulgaria. Many dumbshits, believe it or not. Most important thing? Never give up."

"I think I owe you an apology," Charlie added. "I guess I should take your opinions more seriously. Except for the killing strangers part. And about your ideas on fashion. I mean, your haircut sucks. "

"At least he has hair," Left-Nut said from the peanut gallery.

"Agree to disagree on last point, but sure," Vlad said.

Smokey helped Rob sit up and gave him a hug before shaking Vlad's hand. "Now that you two made out like I knew you would, you can stop with the aggression. What do you say?"

The two former combatants agreed, and Charlie knew he had some making up of his own to do with Sam. He took the boy under his arm and walked him away to apologize in private.

"It appears we're all one big happy dysfunctional family once again. That means it's time to eat," Smokey said.

Even though he had just drowned, Rob agreed the instant he saw the plump turtle. "I'll wait a bit, but I'm down. Never eaten turtle before."

"And I've never cooked it," Katya said. "Maybe just cut some pieces and boil it for stew?"

Vladimir twisted his mouth into a deep frown. "Not acceptable. Propane grill in van. We have turtle steaks in half hour. Get grill going and Vlad start carving turtle."

"I'm on it," Smokey said and headed over, taking the opportunity to bogart a joint along the way. The skill was one he'd always had, and even now something that came as second nature.

Soon everyone had settled down and Vlad set about to deliver on his promise of expertly-cut turtle steaks. First he hung the turtle upside down to let it bleed out, then scrubbed it with the hot water. After removing the shell and guts, the fatty meat went straight to the grill. The smell of it sizzling up was different from what everyone was used to, but their mouths were watering just the same. It was meat after all.

Rob pondered his near-death experience while Katya tended to Sam's injured foot and the others engaged in small talk. Everyone was in good spirits and seemed to be on the same page for once. Even better, the fiasco with Crazy Pat was all but forgotten.

Charlie sat back and watched everyone while chugging down water like he would have once done with beer. Sobriety had been a bit boring, but if he hadn't made the change, it was likely none of them would still be alive.

As he took it all in, a large, skinny dog poked its head out from the nearby forest, drawn by the powerful smell of the grilling meat. The German Shepherd's ears were back and its ribs told the story of extreme hunger.

Before Charlie could say anything, it left the tree line and headed their way. That's when he saw the leash

170

attached to its neck, and the owner attached to the leash. She was a tall woman wearing a torn sun dress and faded Phish shirt. He guessed she was one of the vanished picnickers. She also happened to be a zombie.

The pair made their way towards the camp with haste, hungry for different types of meat. Charlie rose to his feet. "Um, guys, look alive."

Much faster than its owner, the dog practically dragged her behind as they neared the group. Rob was weakened from his ordeal but still strong enough to take the woman down with one swing of his bat. Bloodied but not dead, the woman struggled to rise, and he hit her several more times. A woman that loved Widespread Panic concerts, quinoa salad, and stray animals was finished.

"Losing my touch," Rob said and reached out to pet the dog. It promptly clamped its jaws down on his hand. "Son of a bitch!"

Angered at the attack on its owner, the German Shepherd went berserk, growling and barking as it circled Big Rob. It also had the taste of blood on its lips and was clamoring for more of the same.

Rob poked at it gingerly, not wanting to hurt the dog even after it ripped a good chunk of flesh off his left hand. But it just kept barking.

"Must kill it," Vlad said forcefully. "Too loud."

Rob shook his head as he nudged the starving canine away. "I can't do that, it's a dog for God's sake."

The Bulgarian sighed, took a hit from a joint, and grabbed his knife from the grill. "Vlad not squeamish."

"Hold on, I'll make it leave," Smokey said and grabbed the pot of boiling water. He tossed the hot water at the dog's hind quarters and scored a direct hit, causing a severe burn but saving its life. The dog forgot about her beloved owner and took off for the forest it had come from, shrieking in pain.

"Seriously?" Vlad said with an icy stare. "Better catch

before it brings every zombie in state to our barbecue."

And so Smokey, Vlad, Charlie and the Koreans chased after the dog before it could further ruin their cookout by getting them all killed. They were too late.

As they neared the edge of the forest, a zombie in a tight cheerleading uniform burst from the shadows. Then another and another.

"Nice," Left-Nut said. Then a varsity football team, a special needs water boy and three hundred literally die-hard fans erupted from the woods as well. A whole town, to be precise, and they were headed right for Charlie and company. Crazy Pat had sent them into an ambush.

The Koreans paused to fire every round they had left and then took off, throwing their weapons away. But Pong had waited a second too long and they were right on his heels. He stumbled on uneven terrain, and that was all it took. They dragged the young man to the ground and tore into him without mercy.

But his death bought the others a couple of precious seconds as the mob stopped to feed on the tragic figure. As he reached the camp, still smoking his joint, Vlad grabbed the vodka and propane tank while the others kept right on running down the gravel road. They had nowhere in particular to go, but were going there in a hurry.

Half a mile down the road they spotted a sign for an old graveyard right off the beaten path. Rob was wheezing, Sam was hobbling on his injured foot, and the zombies grew closer by the second. "Go for the graveyard," Charlie said and pointed into the overgrown thicket. "Maybe there's a fence or something."

The others followed, but Vlad stopped running and turned to face the incoming horde. He looped his belt through the vodka bottle's handle and stood shoulder to shoulder with Rob.

"Keep moving!" Charlie said, though he recognized the look of determination on both of their faces.

Vlad set the gas tank down and drew his knife from its sheath while Rob cracked his neck and took a deep breath. "It's go time," he said and nodded to the Bulgarian.

"You got two minutes and then you better come find us," Charlie said and bolted into the forest. Moments later he found the others picking their way through the overgrown graveyard. A fallen fence, tipped over tombstones, and a toppled caretaker's home showed just how dilapidated the place was. But there was a rather large stone mausoleum that appeared to be in excellent shape. Soon, the friends were prying at the entrance door. It was made of iron, it was incredibly rusty, and it was locked from the inside.

Charlie pointed to a set of opaque windows eight feet up. "Smokey, help me boost Sam up and see if he can get in there."

The first window was jammed shut, but Sam was able to work open the second window and climb inside the dusty and smelly building. He slid to the floor and made his way towards the entrance. With just the light from the opened window, it took him a moment to find the door. Now he had to figure out how to unlock it in the dark.

Meanwhile, the bash brothers were having issues of their own — mainly, football-helmet and shoulder-pad-wearing zombies. Rob was swatting them with his bat, but they just kept getting right back up, and his wild swinging was keeping Vlad out of the fray. Luckily the facemasks made it impossible for those particular zombies to bite. But they were swarming the pair, and the other army of zombies closing in had no such handicap.

Vladimir formulated a hasty plan as he pointed to one of the zombie's legs. "Rob slam, Vlad jam."

Rob nodded and hammered the first football player's kneecaps. The Bulgarian instantly pounced and pushed his knife through the fallen teenager's faceguard, burying it to the hilt in the boy's eye socket. Then he rolled over to focus on the next one, already dropped by the other big guy.

This worked great for the first few stragglers, but the main column was coming in and bringing chewed-up death with it.

"Run?" Rob asked as the multitude of zombies got within fifty yards, proving too terrifying even for him.

Vlad stood still. "One more trick up pant leg."

The zombies had closed to twenty-five yards. Vlad sucked one last drag off his joint and spun the propane tank knob to full blast. He placed the cherry in front of the rushing gas.

"*WOOSH!*

Flames shot out ten feet as Vlad's improvised flamethrower ignited without a second to spare. He swung the tank back in forth to create a wall of fire and several zombie cheerleaders burst into flames. But as their ponytails burned off rapidly and their flesh sizzled, the once-adorable cheerleaders kept moving forward, and it wasn't team spirit on their minds.

Rob swung wildly and knocked the trio of flaming teens backwards into the charging throng, where they immediately set others on fire. More took their place and Vlad torched them too while backpedalling away. Then his torch started to flicker.

"Okay, now run."

A voice rang out from the forest. "Sŏ-du-rŭ-se-yo!" It was Ping, shouting at them to hurry.

They followed the Korean soldier through the brush and into the ramshackle cemetery with hundreds of zombies – some flaming – in tow. Charlie was standing at the now-open entrance to the vast mausoleum and screaming profanity-laced encouragement. Ping, then Vlad, and finally Rob shot through the opening as Charlie slammed the door shut. They wedged several steel caskets from the Victorian era against it and waited

174

with baited breath while hands of all shapes and sized pounded on the outside with little success. Charlie and the gang were alive. And trapped. And in the dark.

A bright light radiated outward and bathed the group in an otherworldly glow. It was Smokey's cell phone.

"I kept it charged up for just such an occasion. Plus, I have Tetris on here. Time for you fools to get pwned." Everyone looked at each other in silence for a moment until Left-Nut realized something. "Aw man, Pong was the one I was teaching English. Now I gotta start all over."

Smokey turned his light off, and the fists began to fly from all directions.

*   *   *

An hour passed since the group had become entombed inside the mausoleum, and besides a short-lived Tetris tournament complete with allegations of cheating, they were starting to get unbearably bored.

Left-Nut was nursing a black eye that nobody would fess up to, and that at least was a cause for smiles. But the loss of Pong and their current predicament weighed heavily on everyone. It didn't help that five hundred zombies clamored around the entrance to the mausoleum, pressing in tighter and tighter.

"Think they'll get bored and leave?" Sam asked. Nobody replied, and that was answer enough.

Smokey paced around and chewed on his fingers. "It's like *Sweet Valley High* on mushrooms out there. We're pretty much screwed, chewed, and barbecued."

"Barbecue. I can still smell that turtle cooking on the grill," Rob said. "I bet it would have been delicious."

"That dickhead Pat must have known the zombies were by the lake, too. Not that it matters," Charlie said.

"Creepy jagoff."

"I know this is a long shot, but now would be a great time to pray," Katya suggested. "In the darkest times—"

"No, Sister Buzzkill, now is time to drink," Vlad said. "Time to celebrate life. Didn't save vodka for nothing."

"For once, I agree with him," Charlie added.

Katya nodded. "Okay then. I'll pray, you do your thing. We all have our roles."

And so they began passing the handle of vodka around while telling off-color jokes and stories. Smokey played some music on his phone, and although there was a bit of grumbling about the song selection, it definitely helped them forget their macabre situation. At least a little.

The conversation turned to people that they hoped had died in the apocalypse, including all of the Kardashians, all the world's lawyers, and anyone that said "BOGO" instead of "Buy one, get one."

"Ronald Reagan," Smokey added.

"Man, he's been dead for like, ten years," Charlie said. "Get over it."

"Still, fuck him. War on drugs asshole," Smokey said.

"Speaking of the dead, we should say a few words for Pong," Charlie said. He dumped an ounce of vodka on the floor and continued, "He lived a short, dirty life, and died a horribly violent death. But at least he died free." He patted Ping on the back and handed him the bottle.

The older Korean said a few words and then dumped more vodka out before taking a long pull for himself. He handed the bottle to Rob, closed his eyes, and sat down on the mausoleum floor, lost in his thoughts.

Rob took a massive drink and then ruffled Sam's red hair. "I think it's time for our little guy to have his first drink. It's not like there's a legal age limit anymore. What do you think, Charlie?"

"Sounds like a great idea. Just one drink, though."

Sam looked nervous about the idea and turned to Charlie. "How come you're not joining in? From all the

176

stories it seems like that's all you guys do is drink."

"I used to toss 'em back with the best of them. There were late nights, women, and shenanigans I won't mention in the presence of a nun."

"Thank you," Katya said.

"You could say, for a long time, I was like the dancing gopher in *Caddyshack*. Except when the music stopped playing, everybody else noticed but me. I was in a bad place, trust me. And now I got my head on right for once. So I'll pass, but you go ahead. Your first drink should always be with your best friends."

Sam smiled genuinely at the sentiment and his face turned red even in the dark. He took a quick gulp and coughed most of it up. "This tastes like gasoline. Why would you guys drink this garbage? No thanks."

"Yep, that's what my first time was like," Charlie noted with a grin.

Vlad slapped Sam on the back way too hard. "I take his portion."

The drinking continued and tongues were loosened. Even after his recent anonymous beating, Left-Nut – being Left-Nut – decided to press his luck.

"Doesn't look like we're gonna make it out of here. What do you say, Katya? Fancy a little Cemetery Mary action?"

The nun stood up and quietly walked towards the cretin.

"Oh, hell yes. I didn't think that you'd really take me up on—" He broke off as the nun began to kick his still-injured shin. Repeatedly. "Get off me you damn psycho!"

Big Rob pulled Katya back, although he was purposefully a bit slow to do so. It seemed the day was a good one for kicking Left-Nut's ass, even for members of the clergy

The others roared with laughter at the sight until Charlie cut them off with the wave of a hand. "What's that smell? And I'm not talking about Rob's armpits."

"Smoke," Sam answered as the scent got strong enough

177

for everyone to smell. "It's a forest fire. My scout leader trained us to recognize the smell."

"That must have been a tough one to learn," Left-Nut said and rolled his eyes while rubbing his sore shin.

"He's just trying to help," Smokey said.

"Oh, like you did by burning the dumbass dog half to death?"

"Seriously, you even hate dogs?" Smokey countered.

"No, I don't hate dogs. In fact, I love them. Not that you dick-wads care." Left-Nut sat down Indian-style and went seamlessly into storytelling mode. "We had a poodle that my parents got for my tenth birthday, I named him Elmo and he was my best friend for years."

"I remember that dog, it bit my leg," Rob said.

"He hated everyone except me," Left-Nut said. "And what's with every dog biting you? Is it because you smell like bacon?"

"Okay, so what happened," Charlie said.

"It was Christmas break our junior year of college, and I came home from the bar one night, completely wasted as usual. But you see, Elmo fell asleep at the door waiting for me, and I just didn't see him. I just didn't see him..." Left-Nut attempted to say something else but his words were lost amongst tears, and he broke down like his friends had never witnessed before.

"See, you are a human being after all," Charlie said.

A solitary tear ran down the jerk's face. "I loved that dog. We got him from a puppy mill so he was about half-retarded, but he was a good shit. Little guy followed me around everywhere like I was a rock star."

Rob walked over to a trembling Left-Nut as if he were about to give him a hug. Then he slapped him multiple times. "Pussy!"

"What the hell?"

"You don't get to have feelings after all the shit you've pulled. Nope." It was an odd move for Rob, but there was a bit of justice in it.

"Thank you for sharing," Katya said.

But rather than graciously accept the kind words, Left-Nut returned to true form. "Okay, I'll ask about the five-hundred-pound gorilla in the room that nobody else has the balls to bring up. What happened to your face?"

Katya self-consciously touched her scar before taking a deep breath. "Okay. If you must know, I came to the States from Ukraine after answering an advertisement for students. I thought I would be a nanny, but the men responsible for transit had other ideas."

"I bet they did," Left-Nut said.

"It was a prostitution ring, but one of the gang leaders found out I was a virgin and said he wanted me for himself. He was nicer than the others and told me all I had to do was pay off my tickets and then he would take me away. I would be his girlfriend."

The room was deadly quiet as everyone followed the nun's every word. Except for the zombies banging on the door. They just kept right on hammering away.

"First he had me fill shopping carts with food and then get in line in front of single men. When I couldn't pay, I would cry, and the men would pay for everything. He made me do this all across the city."

"Not a bad scam," Left-Nut said.

Katya nodded. "That was somewhat harmless, but what came next was not. You have seen women begging by subways, holding sleeping children?"

"All the time," Charlie said. "Tossed them a few quarters myself, just to be nice."

"The women are there for many hours, and their babies are always sleeping. How many babies can sleep all day and never cry?"

"I guess I never thought about that. Were they dolls or something?" Charlie asked.

Katya shook her head. "They drugged the children. And people walk right on by, often giving money out of the belief they are helping the children, but only making it worse. Sometimes a woman would overdose her baby and she would have to hold a dead child for hours until another would be brought by as a replacement, like light bulb."

"Jesus," Smokey said. "Sorry. Did that happen to you?"

"Thankfully not on my shift. But after I toiled for six months to repay my debt, the man I trusted brought me to a fancy hotel. I found out he had merely wanted to sell me to the highest bidder. When another man came to claim his prize, I scratched at his face and was beaten in return. They dumped me in an alleyway and splashed Drano on my face."

Charlie thought back to the fateful night of the bachelor party and the Eastern European hooker he'd spent it with. Could she have been in a similar situation, forced into such a life by the very same men? It was a horrible thought, and one he quickly pushed to the back of his mind.

"I promised God that if he saved my life, I would serve him without question," Katya continued, "He did, and here we are."

There was an awkward silence for a while as the heavy story settled in. Then Vlad set the empty bottle down and cleared his throat to change the subject. "Story time over. Now we rest. In morning, we fight."

"You think we can actually make our way out?" Smokey asked.

"Of course not," Vlad answered with a crooked-toothed smile. "But what a glorious death it will be."

Chapter 21
Parting is Such Sweet Sorrow

Russ returned with two gas cans full of diesel fuel after having been gone for a whole day. This was how long it took him to partially sober up and then find his way home from a nearby town after getting extremely ripped off a bottle of Everclear. "Partially" was the key word and it was obvious he was in good spirits. "Did somebody order a taxidermist, because I'm ready to stuff some pus—"

"If anyone needs a taxidermist it's your Betelgeuse-looking ass," Jackie said without even cracking a smile. "Where the hell have you been?"

"Just TCB, baby. Taking care of business."

Padma, however, couldn't contain her grin. "Russ, you are retar-dead. That's all I have to say." For whatever strange reason, the guy was growing on her. He was an idiot for sure, but he had this strange sort of cagey intelligence that she had never seen before. Unlike the professional class Padma had been surrounded with her entire life, Russ was a real man. One that farted and swore, smoked cigarettes and probably cheated in friendly poker games. But they were all alive because of him, and that meant plenty right there.

Russ grinned right back and his greenish tinted eyes, like all the infected had, sparkled with mischief. "If I didn't know better I'd say you missed me."

"But you do know better," Padma countered.

A very different-looking Marquell walked around the corner of the truck and interrupted the banter.

"Carlton Banks," Russ said with a snicker.

"Ain't nobody talkin' to your creepy ass," Marquell said, though there was none of the bitterness the statement might have had days earlier.

"Actually, I like the new hairdo," Russ added.

"Mary did a good job cutting it," Marquell said and ran his fingers through his freshly shorn locks. "But if you must..." To everyone's surprise, he did a spot-on impression of the Carlton Dance from "The Fresh Prince of Bel-Air," complete with a goofy smile. Everyone laughed, and it was clear that Marquell could still be charming on demand.

"Why'd you cut it, though?" Russ asked.

"The dreads were just something I wore for a lawsuit, and also to look hard. And I'm done with that mess."

"How about you put the gas in the truck so we can get going?" Jackie said, cutting the homecoming short. "Hanging out on the highway here isn't exactly inconspicuous, and we've had our fair share of excitement while you were gone." She pointed to a pile of zombie bodies in a nearby ditch.

Russ checked on a sleeping Trent in the back and then did as directed. Soon the semi was travelling down the highway once again, and the airport was just a short ride away. The strange thing was, Russ always drove perfectly fine no matter his B.A.C., and the trip was over in no time.

They pulled up to the abandoned municipal airport and breathed a sigh of relief. It appeared empty, at least superficially, and there were plenty of small planes on the runways. Both major details had been in question before arrival. Now they simply had to find the keys that Marquell promised would be there. And gas up a plane. And actually fly the thing. And land it.

"Morphine's a hell of a drug," Trent said as Padma and Jackie helped him sit down at a red picnic table. The cop was lucid, but moving slow.

"It sure is," Padma said and scratched Elvis tenderly

182

behind her ear. "But you should move as little as possible to avoid breaking your stitches. You aren't out of the woods yet just because it doesn't hurt as much. After all, you only got shot yesterday."

Trent nodded. "Let's not worry about me. Russ and Marquell, get this show on the road. Or in the air, I should say."

The odd couple left the others behind and crept into the main terminal which was little more than a warehouse, and sought out the women's restroom. Marquell walked into the middle stall and stood on the toilet before shoving a ceiling tile up and over. Then he reached inside and felt what he was looking for. Airplane keys. But there were surprises as well. One kilo of shrink-wrapped high-grade Columbian cocaine and a fully loaded 9mm Glock pistol. Only these extra items weren't surprises for Marquell. He grabbed the weapon and clicked the safety off.

Russ was his usual chatty self. "No offense, but—"

Marquell turned and faced Russ, keeping his hand hidden in the ceiling. "Whenever someone says 'no offense,' I know for damn sure what's coming next is gonna piss me right off. So choose your next words carefully."

"I was gonna say, I kinda thought Trent was dumb for saving you at first. But I'm sure glad he did. That's all."

The former gang leader stared ahead, lost temporarily in an inner struggle. He had planned from the beginning to kill Russ and Trent at exactly this juncture, and after the arrival of the women had come up with even worse scenarios.

"You okay bro?"

Marquell nodded his head. "Y'all were dumb for picking up a cold-blooded killer – in reality, a demon." There was a long pause in the conversation as he took the pistol from hiding. "Something with no conscience or soul. Yeah, it was very dumb."

"Now wait just a minute there. You can't—"

"But I guess you got lucky. Because that demon, he's gone." Marquell brought his other hand down and tossed the package of coke to Russ. "Merry fucking Christmas."

"Hot damn, is this what I think it is?"

"Yep." Marquell grabbed the keys and the two rejoined the others at the meeting spot. He placed the pistol on the table as a gesture of goodwill and Russ did likewise with the cocaine.

Trent's eyes grew as big as silver dollars and his nose began to twitch at the sight. "Look who brought the snow to the party."

His trauma doctor noticed the reaction. "Easy there, Steven Tyler," Padma said. "Taking cocaine while on morphine would kill you."

"But oh, what a way to go," Trent said. The cop had been having his own existential crisis after having escaped death a second time – though he was badly wounded – in just the past few days. With nothing but time on his hands he'd been thinking a lot about what drove him to take a bullet for Jackie, a woman he hadn't even known. He kept telling himself it was all about trying to get laid, as lame as that sounded. However, the reality was much different. Like Marquell, he was evolving, in a way. Whether the transformation continued remained to be seen. If his past was any indication, the road to redemption would be quite bumpy indeed.

"Now we have to find a green plane with gold wings," Marquell said. "It's pretty pimp if I do say so myself."

Trent scoffed. "Real subtle for a drug-runner."

Just then, a loud noise startled the group and they looked around in confusion before seeing a large plane coming in for a landing several runways over. Sort of. The landing gear failed to deploy correctly and the plane skidded off the runway and barreled into one of the hangers at high speeds.

A member of the political class, Jackie immediately recognized the white Boeing VC-25 with a distinctive blue stripe running down the middle. It was Air Force One. And it was on fire.

*   *   *

After a moment of shock, everyone except for Trent (who was told to stay at the table) grabbed their improvised weapons and ran towards the wreckage. They were prepared to do something, but they weren't sure what that something was yet.

An evacuation slide inflated and deployed as thick black smoke swirled around the plane while the powerful smell of jet fuel permeated the air. Jackie took the lead. "We'll wait a couple minutes for survivors, but then we better get some distance because this thing could go up. And be ready for zombies to either zip down that slide or come out of nowhere. That wasn't exactly quiet."

A person finally emerged in the doorway and stumbled onto the slide, screaming all the way down before coming to a bloody rest on top of a satchel handcuffed to his wrist. The injured person was followed by a second man that came down shortly after, holding his hands up in surrender.

The first man had a wild fanatical look in his eyes as he stared right through them, speaking like a sidewalk preacher. "The book of Revelations has come true. Babylon the great is fallen, is fallen, and is become the habitation of devils, and the hold of every foul spirit, and a cage of every unclean and hateful bird."

Jackie knew who it was right away, having attended several fundraisers with the injured man. "That's Senator Sanders. My father golfed with him a lot."

The second man, Secretary of State Sam Childers, corrected her. "You mean President Sanders."

185

It was at that point that Russ pounced on the injured man and tore off a huge mouthful of the president's neck, causing blood to shoot outwards like a burst water balloon. Russ's eyes rolled back in his head as he chewed happily on the most powerful man in the world. In response, the president shuddered and involuntarily convulsed in a sickening display.

Everyone else screamed in shock, except for the third man coming down the safety chute. That man promptly shot Russ point blank in the forehead.

Right or wrong, Marquell retaliated and shot the man dead with a blast from his own pistol. In an instant, Stromm Aikens' storied career was ended by the furious pull of a trigger. Marquell fired one more shot into the Secretary of Defense's body before administering the coup de grace on the president.

The whole sequence happened in about thirty seconds, but had changed the trajectory for the course of human history. And to think that Marquell had just devoted his life to doing good deeds.

Padma's lip quivered as she looked at Russ, lying peacefully on the ground, almost appearing alive. "Namaste." She kissed the clean side of his face and said goodbye in her native tongue.

Russ sat up. "What happened?" The bullet was stuck to his forehead and sizzling away like a sausage in a skillet.

"Now that was some *Tango and Cash* shit," Marquell said, not believing his own eyes. "You really do have a hard head."

Russ tapped his bloody noggin and pried the bullet off before tossing it in the grass. "I had a steel plate implanted after a dirt bike accident. Wasn't riding it, the bike just wasn't anchored to the wall right in my garage and it fell on me. They said it would have killed a normal man..."

"Tell stories later, this thing could blow at any second," Jackie said and ushered everyone, including the

Secretary of State, to a safe distance. The plane became completely enveloped in flames but never actually exploded.

Trent was not happy when the situation was explained to him. "I turn my back for one minute and you eat the fucking president? I swear you're crazier than Gary Busey's girlfriend."

"It's not as bad as it seems," the silver-tongued newcomer said.

"And who in Jupiter's balls are you?" Trent asked.

"Sam Childers."

"Doesn't ring a bell."

"You never saw me on CNN? I was kind of a big deal. You know, Secretary of State?"

"CNN's for pussies," Trent said matter-of-factly. "But what are you talking about?"

The man exhaled deeply. "They were horrible men. Totally out of control, and they caused irreparable damage to the world."

"He tasted like mothballs and Viagra," Russ said and spit. "Now Trent's partner, she was delicious. Marquell, your friend wasn't bad, but I'm not into dark meat. Never was."

"Watch yourself," Marquell said with a hard look on his face. "I'm trying to turn over a new leaf here, but I ain't no bitch. Ace was my boy."

"You were just along for the ride?" Padma asked, bringing the subject back to more pressing matters. "You speak of these men like you were an outside observer."

"Actually, yes. They held me captive since the outbreak happened. I was with them, but I wasn't with them, if you catch my drift."

"So why were they keeping you around?" Padma pressed.

"I was smarter than they were and kept them alive. Until we met you..." he said while casting an apprehensive glance in Russ's direction. "And I can pilot a plane.

187

That wasn't me crashing the plane there, by the way."

"No shit? You can fly?" Trent said, turning to Marquell. "That's good news. We were all a little worried about you flying us."

"Me too," Marquell said. "That was my plan's one downfall."

"A pretty big one at that," Jackie added. "Okay, Mr. Secretary. Are you going to fly us out of here then? There's a base in western Illinois we're trying to reach. They have some friends there, and we have a little something else going on too."

"That's Mr. President now," Childers said, noting that he was indeed up in the line of succession. "So it looks like we finally have our first gay president. Not duly elected, mind you, but we'll take what we can get." He looked to Russ. "Do you have a problem with that, Jethro?"

"Course not. One of my best friends was a hom— I mean, gay guy."

The newly minted president was not amused. "And yes, I have thousands of hours under my belt in small aircraft. But you're going to tell me what's going on with this... gentleman, before I agree to help you," he added.

Jackie nodded. "Definitely. I'll fill you in on what's going on and the others can find our plane and see about getting it gassed up."

Her plan was straightforward, but its execution was not. The fuel pump turned up empty, as did their plane, and so they had to siphon fuel from several other planes located all around the airport. By the time this was accomplished the sun had set, and the president convinced them to wait for daylight to begin the next leg of their journey.

The ragtag band huddled together near the truck and asked the man question after question, eager to find out exactly what had happened. For his part, President Childers was happy to oblige, and relished

188

the chance to set the record straight. He told them of the initial outbreak, the nuclear exchange, and the abandonment of their men overseas.

"And the Chinese troops?" Trent asked. "How did they get here?"

"The initial wave caught us unaware because they were pre-positioned in Canada – and even more outrageous, some of our own cities. Chinese Special Forces and saboteurs had very specific orders, and during the chaos of the infection, carried them out to a T."

"My God," Mary said.

"The Chinese called it The Perfect Day, and they modeled it after the sneak attack in Hue, Vietnam."

"I was in Viet—"

"Shut the fuck up, Russ," Trent said.

"Anyway, they'd been studying our weaknesses for years and knew everything about us. They had sniper teams take out half of congress on the first day. But that wasn't even the worst of it. Local government, sheriff's departments, power plant workers... talk about a decapitation strike. And of course, the way they captured cities was horrible. The Rape of Nanking had nothing on the fall of Los Angeles. They marched people right into the sea to save bullets."

"Chicago wasn't exactly a picnic either, buddy," Trent said.

"Of that I have no doubt."

"Why did they do it?" Mary said. "I just don't understand. It's not like we attacked them. We didn't... right? I never really followed the news."

Childers leaned forward. "We didn't attack them first, and we still don't know what precipitated this heinous act. I suppose it's possible they never actually got over the Opium Wars. The Chinese psyche is a very delicate thing, and their culture keeps grudges for a long time."

"Opium Wars, huh?" Trent said, taking a much keener interest in the conversation. "Now there's a war I could get behind."

"I do know the invasion had been planned for some time, and even Mexico was in on it. When our escort plane landed as a decoy, they blew it up on the tarmac. We've been hiding out ever since, going from one Podunk to the next as our numbers dwindled. The plane's lack of proper maintenance finally caught up with us, not to mention the fact that the runway here was too small."

"Do you have any idea what caused it? The virus or whatever it is that's turning people into—"

"Zombies," Russ said emphatically, interrupting Padma.

President Childers nodded. "We had trouble finding out for weeks until an isolated research center got back to us. You're right that it is a virus. What's interesting is what the virus does. You see, it shuts down an area of the brain called the claustrum, and thereby disables consciousness. Chinese scientists made some type of artificial chromosome and attached it to—"

"Boring!" Russ interrupted again.

Flummoxed, the president decided story time was over and retreated to a separate picnic table to gather his thoughts. The night wore on, and one by one the members of the group dozed off while the president kept a watchful eye on Russ. When Jackie ultimately went into the cab to sleep, Russ was left on watch since he no longer had the urge or need to sleep. Plus he felt like drinking some more. He always did.

President Childers called the former truck driver over and immediately began to grill Russ about his "situation." Of course, this was a topic Russ loved to pontificate about, so as the liquor flowed freely, so too did the conversation.

Russ talked about his truck driving, his ex-wives, and how he became infected. The president was especially interested in all of the super duper powers Russ picked up after said infection, particularly his ability to travel unnoticed by other zombified individuals.

A plan soon formed in President Childers's head and he had just a few more questions to ask. "You said you've travelled the entire country. Did your wanderings ever take you through Wyoming?"

"Sure did. I know Wyoming like the back of my nuts," Russ said and took a swig of the rapidly disappearing Everclear. "Used to haul freight through it for years, back before my license got yanked."

"Then you're probably familiar with the Yellowstone Lake area?"

"Like the front of my nuts," Russ said. "Caught a shitload of cutthroat trout there. Out of season. That's just how I roll."

"If I get you close, can you help me find the West Thumb spot?"

"Yep."

"Excellent. That's where we're headed. Just the two of us. We'll fly out immediately."

"For what?" Russ asked.

The president looked him square in the eye. "Russell, your country needs you." He pointed to the truck. "They need you. We're gonna end this war."

"But why can't my friends come with?" Russ asked.

"We require a light footprint. And your special... talents are just what's required to get the job done."

The speech tugged perfectly on Russ's patriotic heartstrings and played into his delusions of grandeur at the same time. "Sir, let's fucking do it." He saluted the president and then walked over by his friends to say a quiet goodbye.

Russ found Padma sleeping in the front seat and put his hand softly to the window, peering at the dark-skinned beauty for a moment. "Parting is such sweet sorrow, that I'll say good night until tonight becomes tomorrow." Russ put his head down and walked away, his eyes clouding over. "Kinda liked her."

"That's from 'Romeo and Juliet,'" the president said. "I'm impressed."

Russ nodded. "Yeah, I have the porno version memorized."

There was an awkward pause as the president began questioning his own sanity. He got over it. "Um, let's go."

*   *   *

The next morning it quickly became clear that the group had shrunk by two members and one airplane. Trent and Marquell went ballistic while the women searched for clues. It didn't take them long to find one.

A note was written on the picnic table in what was most likely Russ's blood. Padma read the message aloud, shrinking in embarrassment with each line.

Padmay,

It is with great sorrow that I must inform you I have been called to serve a higher purpose (have to save the world and stuff). I know we didn't have a lot of time together, but I feel fortunate to have met you even under such dire circumstances. And although Indian food always gave me the shits, I found you to be one tasty treat. See you in the afterlife. Oh, and the prez says whatever you do, don't cross the Mississippi.

Russ Kaminsky,
Zombie Samurai

"He spelled your name wrong," Jackie said as Padma continued to stare at the note, oddly moved by the Civil War-sounding letter.

"So what do we do now?" Mary said. "They took the

only plane we had the keys for."

Jackie pointed to the semi. "I suppose we try and locate some diesel and then load up the ol' 'Flaming Cowboy' again. I know the roads aren't safe, but at this point we don't have other options. Does anyone know how to drive that thing?" Negative. "Okay, so then we'll have to learn."

Suddenly, Trent got very, very mad. "Hey, where's the coke?"

Chapter 22
Dawn of the Deadbeats

Charlie and the group awoke to the sound of crows squawking in unison as the tiniest bit of sunlight crept through the mausoleum windows. Surprisingly, every one of them had achieved a good night's sleep. Maybe the alcohol had something to do with it, or even the threat of imminent death combined with being surrounded by solid walls for once. If you're going to die anyway, you might as well get a good night's sleep.

Whatever reason it was, the gang rubbed the sleep from their eyes and gathered up their rudimentary weapons. On the other side of the door were several hundred infected townsfolk with nothing to do but wait.

Vlad swished the last of the bottle of vodka like mouthwash and then swallowed it with a grin. "Breakfast of champions."

"Gross," Smokey said and spit on the floor, his own mouth tasting of cheap vodka from the previous night.

"Not Vlad's fault you drink like bunch of Czech schoolgirls."

Smokey shrugged. "Is that an insult or a compliment? I'm still having a hard time telling what's what with you."

Charlie decided there was no point waiting around now that they were well rested, and decided to give an impromptu pep talk. "We've made it too far just to die like this. I have to believe it's for some reason."

"Agreed," Katya said.

"Which means we're gonna bust right on out of here. Rob, Vlad, and myself will lead the way and everyone else make a break for it, right into the forest. If you get split up, head straight west. He looked to Rob and clarified. "Which is the opposite of the sun right now. I know there's a river ahead like five or ten miles, so wait for the others there. But don't wait long." They moved the steel caskets from the door and paused while Charlie looked at each group member in the eyes, maybe for the last time. "We can do this. Ready?"

They nodded in unison and the crew prepared to sally forth from the doorway in one last valiant charge, with Vlad getting a chance at that magnificent death he had sought for so long.

Rob pulled the door open, bounded out... and fell down with a crash. He had tripped on a pile of badly burned bodies that had been resting against the mausoleum. Lots and lots of dead bodies, with Pong's corpse amongst them.

It seemed the flaming zombies had ignited the surrounding forest, killing the rest of the mob with the one-two punch of fire and smoke inhalation. The creatures simply weren't smart enough to flee the path of the flames, and as they had crowded together outside the mausoleum, they all died where they stood. Every last one of them.

"You see," Katya said. "Someone is looking out for us."

Charlie pointed to Pong's body. "We should bury him and be on our way. It's the right thing to do."

"We can use my shovel," Katya said.

For once, Left-Nut had a good idea. "How about we put him in one of those coffins in the mausoleum? It might be a tight fit, and he'll have some company, but it will save a lot of time." Everyone agreed, and they set about making it happen.

Minutes later, Seung Sahn, also known affectionately as Pong, a nineteen-year-old soldier born and raised six thousand miles away in the industrial city of Chongjin, was laid to rest. He would share eternity with a pig-tailed seventeen-year-old girl from the prairie, killed by a fever long ago. Neither had ever had the chance to grow up or fall in love, but both would never be alone again.

Meanwhile, Vladimir checked over the townsfolk and found several that were still technically alive, despite being horribly disfigured. So Vlad pulled a rusty axe from a nearby tree stump and put them out of their misery with gruesome efficiency. The Bulgarian whistled as he worked, and didn't break a sweat.

*   *   *

"Okay, pledge, on to the next lesson," Left-Nut said to Sam. "Let me tell you about why I love fat chicks so much. It comes down to body temperature regulation. They're warm in the winter and shady in the summer. Then you have your chanky girls. Those are the chunky slash skanky hybrids I told you about. It's a killer combo for sure."

The boy was the last one willing to walk by Left-Nut at this point. Because of this he had become a captive audience over the past several hours as they plodded along yet another deserted country road.

There was only so much Rob could listen to. "Just leave him alone. He shouldn't be hearing your garbage."

"Garbage? Someone has to carry on my traditions after I'm gone. There's a lot of wisdom contained underneath this crown of whiteness."

"Yeah, you're a real national treasure," Rob said.

"Left-Nut's a jerk. Left-Nut's always whacking off. Left-Nut banged Gay Mike," Left-Nut said mockingly.

"Dude, all those things are true," Smokey said.

Left-Nut huffed. "Regardless, I'm sick of being everybody's butt-monkey. I get no respect."

"Reft-Nut cranky," Ping said, putting a few of the English words he knew to good use.

196

"Suck it, Ping. With teeth like that I bet you could eat corn through a picket fence."

"Leave him out of this," Smokey said. "He doesn't even know what you're saying. And I wouldn't be making fun of anyone's appearance if I looked like a Benjamin Button version of Don Flamenco."

"Hey, you know I got struck by lightning. Low blow."

But now Smokey was on a roll. "Guess who else only had one ball? Hitler."

"Going Godwin on me?" Left-Nut said, feigning indignance. "But seriously, why am I always the pivot man in the circle-jerk?"

"Guys drop it," Charlie said from up ahead. They were fewer than twenty miles from home and he was running low on energy and patience. The closer they got to their destination, the farther away it seemed.

"This is an A B conversation so... shut the fuck up," Left-Nut said with a crappy Captain Kirk impersonation. Like usual, he seemed to be enjoying the confrontation.

But Charlie was not. He stopped walking, turned, and got into his friend's face. "Fine. I'm sick of this shit. This is like the third time we've had this conversation so I'm just gonna lay it on the table. You are completely and utterly worthless. All you are is a mouth that whines, talks shit, complains, and eats. You don't fight, you don't scout, and you don't cook. No, all you do is bitch and annoy." Charlie turned to the others. "Am I right? Anyone want to speak up for him?" They spoke up all right, but not in his defense. "See, the tribe has spoken."

"Like I give two shits," Left-Nut said softly. "A tribe of fuckin' losers."

"Okay then, if you're so keen to pass on your knowledge, let's tell Sam about what you did on senior night."

"That's not necessa—"

"Oh, but it is," Charlie said and looked to Sam. "The other football team had a player with downs, and both teams worked out a deal beforehand to let him score at the end of the game." He pointed at Left-Nut, who was shrinking before their eyes. "But this dickweed sacks the kid and returns the fumble for a touchdown as the clock expired. Spiked the football, moonwalked, and it was game over."

And then Left-Nut exploded. "Fuck him, I regret nothing! That was my last chance to score a touchdown, too!"

"And that's why you don't take his advice on anything," Charlie said and retook his position at the front of the caravan.

Left-Nut was silent for the rest of the day, and it was clear Charlie's comments had struck a nerve.

*　　　　　*　　　　　*

The next morning, Charlie had everyone up and moving before the sun even rose. He was cheerful, there was a spring in his step, and he was cautiously optimistic about what the coming day would bring.

An hour later the others caught his spirit as they came upon row after row of blueberry bushes. The field had been left to nature, but what the birds and deer had left behind could have fed an entire army. Or a dozen Big Robs.

"These are better than I remember," he said after stuffing the umpteenth monster handful into his mouth. "We used to work here during the summer," he said to Katya and then continued to gorge, his beard stained blue from excess juices. "Best job ever. I ate so many blueberries one time my poop turned blue for a week."

"Cool story, bro," Left-Nut said.

Rob answered with a blast of blueberries to Left-Nut's face, and soon everyone else was tossing the tart berries in all directions as an all-out food fight erupted. Even

Left-Nut joined in and soon the trials of the day before were but a memory.

Charlie launched a bunch of berries at Katya, who promptly dodged and fired some back, nailing him in the face. She laughed vigorously at the high jinx and Charlie noticed for the first time just how attractive she was, burned face and all. Katya had the heart-shaped face, defined lips, and striking cheekbones common amongst Ukrainian women, but she also had an inner splendor that matched. Charlie pushed such thoughts aside and filled his pockets with the delicious bounty before ordering everyone onwards.

The surprise breakfast had been fun, but they were now less than a mile from his parents' house. With a possible family reunion so tantalizingly close, Charlie could barely keep from running ahead on his own. As the dawn peaked above the eastern horizon, he dared to believe a happy ending was possible. And then he saw his old asshole neighbors.

The Johnson boys, A.J and B.J., were in the middle of the road, shooting pigeons off a telephone wire and laughing hysterically. "The cables line 'em up real good," the older one said and adjusted his Red Sox hat.

"Won't be fun picking the buckshot out," B.J. said.

"Exactly, that's why you'll be doing it," A.J. answered, then turned to greet the newcomers. "Get the fuck off my land!"

"I'll handle this," Charlie said as he approached his childhood neighbors with Vlad and Smokey flanking him. The men before them were bullies, loudmouths, and perennial d-bags — so pretty much exactly the type of person Charlie was used to dealing with.

"We're just passing through, Andrew. No need for hostilities."

"Charlie Campbell, in the flesh. Glad to see you're balder than Vin Diesel's balls."

"Nice to see you too, buddy."

A.J. was far from finished. "Nice beards on the rest of you dingleberries. What, are you guys hipsters now?"

"And they're dressed for Halloween," B.J. said, piping up like the toady he'd always been.

Charlie stifled an angry response that disparaged both Bill Buckner and A.J.'s mother. "Razors... have been a little tough to come by. But that's not important. Like I said, we're just passing through."

"I'd need sheep shears to man-scape at this point," Left-Nut said to nobody in particular.

Charlie tried to pass, but A.J. moved to block him. "Where the fuck do you think you're going, Romeo?"

Now Charlie's temperature was starting to rise. "I'm going home. Now the sooner you get out of the way, the sooner you can get back to your Duck Dynasty reach around or whatever it is you're doing out here."

"Now you did it," B.J. said as his brother's face turned beet-red.

"You and I have unfinished business, Charlie."

"Which is?"

A.J. bristled, and he raised his shotgun ever so slightly. "Like you don't know. You stole my girlfriend, asshole."

The conversation had turned from bizarre to ridiculous, and Charlie clenched his fists tightly. "Oh for fucks' sake, that was like fifteen years ago. I had a full head of hair and I liked Limp Bizkit back then, too. Times have changed."

"Now you're saying you did it all for the nookie? Trying to rub my face in it, city boy?"

"No, what's wrong with you, man?"

B.J. laughed nervously and raised his own shotgun. "Bend over and lube up those bungholes, boys, you're about to get plowed."

Then it was Vlad's turn to chuckle. "Very bold, but only making noise. Like way rooster is king of barn until brought to chopping block."

A.J. looked at Vlad with a scowl, but then his face brightened as he recognized the former world champion. "Holy shit, it's the Dragon!" He moved closer. "Man, I gotta shake your hand. That was priceless when you kicked Big Rob's ass. Fat bastard had it coming. He knocked me and B.J. out at a cookout one time."

"He did have it coming," Vlad answered. And then it happened. Quickly. Vlad's knife sliced through A.J.'s throat like hot butter and found its way into B.J.'s heart in one graceful motion.

The two brothers looked at each other in confusion before collapsing upon one another in a final embrace. It was quiet except for the sound of blood streaming onto the pavement, puddling around a dead pigeon.

Charlie's jaw dropped. "Jesus Christ, I used to play hide and seek with those guys. You're like a goddamned Michael Myers or something."

"Is Austin Powers, right?"

"No, the killer, you dumbfuck," Charlie said, still trying to process the violence as the others ran up to them.

"Never heard of him." Vlad pulled the blade from the dead man's chest and then wiped it clean on the B.J.'s acid-washed cutoff jean shorts.

Charlie looked at the bodies and shook his head. It was clear Vlad was too much of a loose cannon, and he had to go. "You know this just isn't—"

He stopped midsentence as something caught his eye. Charlie bent over and picked the shotgun up as his heart sank like a stone. There was a familiar inscription engraved on the side plate – an inscription from his mother to his father. The two dead men were instantly forgotten as Charlie sprinted towards home. So close, and yet so far away.

Minutes later Charlie gasped for air as he stopped in front of his parents' isolated house. Crickets chirped loudly in the overgrown bean fields as he searched for anything out of the ordinary. From the outside the place looked exactly as he remembered it, and Charlie hoped against hope for a simple explanation. Maybe his father traded the shotgun, or maybe he sold it?

He walked down the gravel driveway towards the front door and absentmindedly looked into his sister's station wagon that was parked there. Big mistake.

Charlie's sister, Melody, was nowhere to be seen. But her son, a precocious two-year-old named Cody who often claimed his boogers were cookie crumbs, was still strapped into his seat. At least, the lower half of him was. The rest had been ripped away and digested long ago.

The sight was too much, and Charlie violently puked before crying out in anguish. Then he wiped his mouth and stormed inside the house before the others could stop him. Not surprisingly, what he found within was just as bad.

They say you can never go home, and during a zombie apocalypse, this is more often true than not. The house had been ransacked and the back screen door banged open and shut with the breeze. It appeared wildlife had moved in some time ago. And the smell was about as bad as expected. Sour. Wet. Dead.

However, the dilapidated state of the home wasn't what bothered Charlie now. His mother was on the living room floor where her decomposing body was slowly melting into the shagged carpet. Melody was several feet away and in the same condition, but with a gunshot through her head and pants around her ankles. Charlie did not even want to think about whatever chain of events had led to such a scene.

And then, as he looked up, he came face to face with his father. Or, more aptly, what used to be his father. The infected man had come up from the basement as Charlie wept loudly, and was now heading right for him.

Without hesitating, Charlie swung his dad's shotgun overhead like a club and brought the man low. He slammed the butt down again and again until his father's face resembled a spilled bowl of tomato soup. It was an inglorious end for such a kind soul, and that made it all the more horrible.

The others ran inside, and Charlie, covered in his own father's blood and gore, turned to Katya with a cold glare. "How come nobody was looking out for them too?"

There was absolutely nothing Katya could say at that moment, so she grabbed Sam and quietly slipped out the back door. As unhinged as he was – and rightfully so – she wasn't sure what Charlie was about to do. But she did know that Sam shouldn't see it.

Muttering to himself, Charlie dragged the bodies into a pile, albeit gently, and closed their eyes while staring intently at each family member. He tried to focus on happy family memories, as if that could somehow alleviate the pain. However, nothing could block out the reality of the hellhole in front of him.

Having been raised by the Campbells due to his own dysfunctional family, Rob was almost as upset as Charlie. The big man would have collapsed into a blubbering pile of despair had Ping and Smokey not supported him. Even so, each trembling sob threatened to bring all three down to the ground.

Charlie grabbed a knit blanket from the couch and walked outside, quickly coming back with his nephew's desiccated remains. He gently placed the blanket on his sister's lap and then went to his own childhood bedroom, returning moments later with a handful of cardboard boxes. It was his baseball card collection, the ultimate symbol of youth and innocence. Those days were gone for good. For everyone.

The distraught son, brother, and uncle began piling the cards on top of his family in a bizarre funeral pyre. He threw unopened packs of Donruss into the mix, loose cards he never got around to sorting, and then his 1987 Tops complete set, the one with the brown borders. It was from the last year he collected the cards before they became uncool. Next came a stack of rookie cards for his favorite players including Bo Jackson, Ozzie Smith, and of course, Nolan Ryan. For some reason Charlie gripped the card tightly as he pictured the time the old pitcher beat the crap out of Robin Ventura for charging the mound.

He took the lighter from Smokey and torched the card, letting the flames lick his hand before dropping it into the pile.

*   *   *

The group left the house after it became fully engulfed in flames and marched silently through the forest towards their final destination. Charlie's optimism from earlier in the morning had been replaced by utter and abject despondency. If bad news greeted him at the base, he was likely to end it all right there.

The loss of Charlie's family had been a heavy blow, but with mere miles separating them from the alleged base, their plans moving forward needed to be addressed. Still smarting from his dressing down the day before, Left-Nut took it upon himself to broach the subject all the same.

"I know it sucks, Charlie. But we should look ahead here. It's painful, I get it, but—"

"Don't pretend you know what I'm going through," Charlie said without slowing down.

Left-Nut moved in front of him. "Look at me. Look at them. All our families are dead too. We just didn't have to see it."

"Mine's not," Vlad said.

"Shut the fuck up," Left-Nut shot back, using the phrase on someone else for once. "Far be it from me to be the voice of reason, but if there's one thing I'm good at, it's self-preservation. And I'm telling you, we need to get

204

it together and fast. I mean, do we think they're just gonna let us waltz right into this military base? Do we think they'll like us showing up with one of the *enemy?*"

"Ping is one of us," Sam said.

"They don't know that," Left-Nut replied. "Hell, they might shoot us on sight just for fraternizing with him."

"So what are you saying?" Charlie asked.

Left-Nut lowered his voice. "I'm saying we need to think this through and try to put a more diplomatic spin on things here. Our meeting with the Johnson boys didn't go too swell now did it? Just like our run-in with Crazy Pat, though I'll take the blame for that one."

"They killed my family."

"Possibly, but we didn't know it at the time Vlad cut them up like Thanksgiving leftovers. I'm just saying, you're obviously pissed right now, and deservedly so. How about we let cooler heads prevail when we get there? I'd say Smokey does the talking."

For once, the long-haired stoner nodded in agreement with Left-Nut. "He's a bastard, but he's right on this. As of now, I'm in charge. Ping will just stay back a ways until we defuse the situation." He looked at Vlad. "And no bullshit out of you."

"What? I am like stray kitty cat."

There was a collective eye roll and they took off again, at least with some semblance of a plan this time. As they worked their way through the trees, nobody knew what lay ahead, but they all understood things were about to change for better or worse.

Thirty minutes later the guessing game was over. "Guys, we're here," Rob said and waved them up to his position on the edge of the forest.

The sight that greeted them was not what they had expected. Instead of an actual military base, the fort was a massive shipping facility surrounded by vast walls of sandbags. Heavy machine guns were visible on the roof and only one road led to the main gate, with a charter bus parked in front of it. In an ominous sign, the surrounding field was littered with hundreds, if not thousands, of rotting corpses and random body parts.

"Zombies?" Rob said.

"Maybe," Left-Nut answered. "Or maybe they were assholes like us sneaking up to a secret military base."

"Guess we'll find out," Smokey said and took his wife-beater undershirt off, attaching it to a nearby stick. "Don't worry, I've seen shit like this a million times on television. The important thing is to stay confident and speak in a direct but nonthreatening manner. I'll go straight up to the side wall and work my way over to the main entrance."

Without further ado, Smokey started the hundred-yard walk across the field of death, stopping every so often to wave his white flag to avoid being mistaken for a canni-bal. Only a chorus of crows, angry at the interruption of their feast, greeted his arrival.

Soon he had reached the wall, but something wasn't right. For starters, he should have been spotted by the sentries well in advance. Upon closer inspection, it became apparent why he hadn't been. The watchmen were skeletons.

Smokey set the stick down and waved at his friends.

"It's a ghost town, come on over!"

Big mistake. Dozens of zombies came streaming out from behind the back side of the fort with extreme prejudice. Smokey had been lulled into a false sense of security by the deaths of the countless zombies around him, and he would now likely pay for it.

The others were too far away to do anything but watch in horror as the pack descended upon their friend. Smokey looked at his stick, threw it on the ground and fumbled for the last joint tucked away in his underwear. The killers got within fifty yards as he pulled the joint out and prepared to light it.

Boom! Boom! Boom boom boom!

Smokey dropped his Grateful Dead lighter as the zombies detonated by the handful, having run straight into a minefield. He had somehow managed to walk through it unscathed, but the cannibals were not as fortunate, and Bouncing Betty fragmentation devices were blowing them up like moist fireworks.

The rest of the group hugged the edge of the forest and made their way towards the road. They reached it safely while the zombies continued to explode in the field.

Eventually, the last of the runners, an elderly woman, hobbled towards Smokey with great effort but minimal speed. She detonated into nothingness several yards from her target, showering Smokey in dentures and old lady parts, but leaving him otherwise unharmed.

As the smoke cleared, a semi pulled down the lone road and stopped in front of the group, and they clenched their weapons in anticipation of whatever clusterfuck was next.

The passenger door opened, and after a few painful seconds of waiting, a heavily bandaged man limped around to the front, carrying a clipboard.

"Can I get somebody to sign for this delivery of two thousand dildos?" Trent said.

Laughing heartily, Smokey pointed his thumb at Left-Nut. "No man, we've got plenty of dildos already."

As Trent's group exited the vehicle, Left-Nut shook his head in amazement at Smokey. "I'd say you're luckier than Justin Bieber's dick right now."

"Hey, I did win the lottery, remember?" Smokey said with a grin and stepped forward to grab his lighter.

Click. He looked down just as the landmine shot up from the ground.

"Bummer," Smokey said while the explosion of shrapnel and death enveloped him. His fabled luck had run out.

*   *   *

Trent's happy reunion had been short-lived due to Smokey's sudden demise. But life, and the struggle to maintain it, had to go on. After a brief burial of the parts of Smokey's body that had been blown into the safety of the road, the merged group climbed on top of the semi and made their way inside the looming base.

As expected, it was completely abandoned. The place also appeared to have been evacuated in a hurry as plenty of supplies and weaponry seemed to have been left behind. This was little comfort for anyone at this point, but it was better than nothing.

Marquell and Jackie took a group and set about gathering those resources while Charlie, Left-Nut and Rob searched for clues about the evacuation.

After two hours of searching, they still had nothing. Charlie was about to give up when Sam came to them holding a piece of paper.

"This might be something. I found it on a bulletin board by the kitchen. You said you were looking for a child, right?" Sam handed over a crudely drawn picture.

"Wow, great work," Left-Nut said sarcastically. "Let's put it up on the fridge."

But Charlie smiled broadly. "That's Brandon's. I'd recognize his shitty drawings anywhere." The picture showed a small black child up in a tree surrounded by what looked like bucktoothed vampires. Also in the picture was a man in a red outfit who looked like a bald superhero, his arms reaching upwards. It was Charlie.

"Why's he wearing a football helmet?" Rob asked.

"Huh? That is strange," Charlie said and looked closer. Indeed, the Brandon in the drawing was wearing a Denver Broncos football helmet, and the helmet had been drawn much better than the rest of the picture, possibly by an adult's hand. "I think it's a clue. Maybe they weren't allowed to leave us a message, but they did anyways."

"And?" Trent said.

"And we're going to Denver. Might even be able to catch them along the way. We should hurry up."

Left-Nut exhaled deeply. "We barely made it halfway across the state and now you want to try and cross half the country in some sort of *Lord of the Rings*-type caper?"

"Yes," Charlie said flatly.

"All based on a fucking hunch? And for argument's sake, what if we find the base and everyone's dead?" He was interrupted as a giggling Vladimir walked by like a kid in a candy store, draped in ammo belts and carrying a .50 caliber Browning machine gun. Left-Nut ignored him. "Or what if your girlfriend's moved on from your pathetic, pining ass? I've seen enough Maury Povich to know that just because you're baby's daddy doesn't mean you get the keys to the castle. She could be knocking combat boots with half the National Guard by now. Fuck, she's might not even be pregnant. I mean, how well do you actually know her? It wouldn't be the first time you got suckered by a chick."

Charlie could ignore Left-Nut's diatribe except for the last part. The truth was he didn't know Brooke all that well. If she had used him, she got exactly what she wanted: a one way ticket out of shithole Chicago. But there was a flicker of hope still alive for Charlie, and for the rest of them. And he was going to seize it.

An ominous rumbling was suddenly heard far away in the distance, accompanied by the telltale sounds of gunfire. It was coming from tanks. Lots and lots of them. And now they knew why the base had been evacuated.

"You got something better to do?" Charlie asked, arching an eyebrow.

"No," Left-Nut replied.

"That's what I thought."

Epilogue

Russ had remained quiet for a full thirty minutes as the president piloted the aircraft in similar silence. Ahead were dark skies and darker thoughts.

Finally, the truck driver could take it no longer. "Time for some Columbian marching powder," he said and pulled the kilo of cocaine out from underneath his seat. Next he cut a small hole in the plastic with his pocket knife. The knife went to his nose and Russ snorted long and hard. "Yikes. That's some good shit."

"I hardly think that's what we need at the—"

"It's gonna keep me from eating you in the near future," Russ said. "Plus, I like to party yo."

"I suppose we can't have that," the president said, his eyes lingering on the contraband.

Russ instinctively lined the gentleman up with his own bump and President Childers took it like a champ. "That is good shit," he said and refocused on flying. But the drug had already loosened his tongue, and soon the reserved politician was spilling his guts. He told Russ about the war, how big of a prick the former president had been, and even about his childhood.

Amped up on weasel dust, Russ was a surprisingly good listener. But he had topics he wanted to discuss as well.

"You know all the insider info right?"

"You could say I was privy to top-secret information, before and after the outbreak. What are you getting at?"

"Conspiracies and stuff," Russ said. "Come on, you gotta tell me some of 'em. Was the moon landing real? What about Bigfoot?"

The new president sighed. "Okay, just one. Have you seen those cash for gold stores? It turns out the government was secretly behind them. We sold all the gold in Fort Knox years ago when prices were high. But we wasted the money and then we had to scrape together new bars when Germany wanted their own ones back from the federal vaults. It was a huge—"

"No, man. I'm talking about aliens, Bermuda Triangle, stuff like that," Russ said, not bashful in the least bit about cutting the leader of the free world off midsentence.

"Fine. NASA detected distant alien life in 2010 and the government was planning to give full disclosure in 2020. Not anymore..."

"Ha, I knew it," Russ said. "If there are zombies, there might as well be aliens too. Reminds me of the time I was hauling chickens through Kentucky and saw a flying saucer shoot right over my rig. Was hoping I'd get beamed up to wang-bang some green hotties or something. Of course, I was blitzed off trucker speed, some ludes, and a sixer of Old Mil. So it might have been a crop duster for all I know."

"Yes, indeed," President Childers said and chuckled to himself about his white lie. Due to the chemicals coursing through his veins he was definitely feeling better than he had for a long while. "This would be a great time for a selfie."

"Selfie? Is that when you try to blow yourself? Never could master the skill. Not that I didn't try."

"No, Russell. It's when you take a picture of yourself and then post it online for others to look at. I just thought it would be interesting to see the president of the United States flying with a zombie co-pilot while high on cocaine. Forget I mentioned it."

And so the discussion went on like that for quite a while, but there was a method to the president's madness. He was enjoying the conversation with the country bumpkin but was also mentally evaluating his new companion at the same time. The results were not spectacular. However, desperate times called for desperate measures. There was a lot of that going on lately.

Having sufficiently gauged Russ's mental acuities, President Childers tried to relax and let his exquisite mind wander. This created an awkward lull in the conversation for about thirty seconds, and Russ would not stand for it.

"Man, I loved hauling freight. The freedom of the wide open road, the God-given beauty of America's wilderness. The hookers."

"Sounds lovely."

"Speaking of hauling," Russ said while digging into the white bag once more. "Any chance I could get my driver's license back? With like a get out of jail free card? You are the president."

"A pardon?"

"Did you fart?" Russ asked.

"No, not pardon me, a *pardon*. It's like you said, a get out of jail card."

"Sure, whatever you want to call it. I just wanna drive again when this whole thing blows over. Best time of my life was on the road."

"Russell, I'll be frank with you. An alcoholic zombie has no business behind the wheel of any vehicle, much less a forty-ton truck possibly hauling hazardous or explosive material. So no, you won't be getting your license back."

"Dang."

"But it doesn't matter, because this trip we're going on... it's one way for both of us."

Russ's creepy green eyes narrowed. "How so?"

"I said I didn't know why we got invaded, but that wasn't entirely accurate. You see, China was gripped by famine as its fields dried up and blew away. It made the Dust Bowl look like nothing. Their land, once sacred to
212

them, became worthless, and the rest of the world shrugged."

"I'm listening," Russ said and did another bump. For safety precautions, of course.

"Which leads me to the opinion that they didn't come here for the love of conquest or retribution. They came here to eat."

"Like a bear coming into a campsite?" Russ said.

"Exactly. Take away the food, i.e. the breadbasket of the U.S., and the bear goes elsewhere. So that's what we're going to do, more or less. They have no supply line whatsoever, so we're talking a Napoleon in Russia scenario here."

President Childers pointed to an inconspicuous satchel in the corner of the plane. He had sawed it off the former president's hand right before they left. "That's a backpack bomb. An Atomic Demolition Munition to be precise. We're going to take it inside an observation tunnel heading into the Yellowstone caldera." Russ looked confused and the president clarified. "It's a giant super volcano. We set it off and it covers half the country in ten feet of radioactive ash. That's why I had you tell your friends not to cross the Mississippi. It's called the Sampson Option, and it will end the war."

"Jesus. But we'll wreck half the country, won't we? That kinda sucks."

"Do you have a better idea Russell?"

"Of course not. Kind of a man of action over here."

The president softened his tone. "Look, the super volcano is going to blow up sooner or later anyway. Maybe next year, maybe next decade. We already paid Brazil billions to build temporary housing as a contingency plan. It doesn't look like we'll need it, though."

Russ's ever-present grin had disappeared as he set the cocaine down and tipped his bottle of rapidly disappearing whiskey. Even the drink could not tame the goose bumps on his hairy arms.

"It's not all bad, though. You might end up saving the world. What will be left of it, anyway."

The patented grin returned. "Hah, and some of my ex-wives said I'd never amount to shit."

"What did the other ones say?" the president asked.

"Who knows? They had restraining orders out on me."

It was the president's turn to grin. "They were wrong about you, Russell. Dead wrong."

The conversation was over and the two very different men pondered what tribulations were ahead. Dawn broke soon after, and the skies turned a beautiful pink while the small plane soared over the fallow fields below, carrying one president, one knucklehead, and one last chance for humanity.

About The Author

Richard Johnson (sort of) grew up in the small-town of Galesburg, Illinois during the 80s. He currently lives with his thriving family outside of Chicago, where he is a full-time parent and part-time yorkie wrangler/duck whisperer.

Richard is a self-acclaimed expert of the zombie genre and is the author of the wildly popular Dead Drunk series, with titles including "Dead Drunk: Surviving the Zombie Apocalypse... One Beer at a Time," "Dead Drunk II: Dawn of the Deadbeats," and "Weekend At Vidu's... a Dead Drunk Short."

Richard is a good friend, a bad cook, and a terrible dancer. If there is ever a real zombie apocalypse (fingers crossed), seek him out for advice and comic relief. But bring plenty of beer.

Check Out "Weekend At Vidu's... A Dead Drunk Short"

Vidu, a used car dealer and d-bag extraordinaire, had been aimlessly wandering the streets of Chicago with only one thing on his mind... and that was before he got turned into a zombie.

Just when you thought you had seen the last of him, now you can find out what happened to Vidu after he left his friends behind during the pandemonium of "Dead Drunk: Surviving the Zombie Apocalypse... One Beer at a Time." Humor, action, zombies, hangovers, gratuitous insults, and more Vidu!

This short story can be read as bonus material for fans of the Dead Drunk series, or as an introduction to the Dead Drunk world, where the only thing with more bite than the zombies are the jokes.

Credits

I would like to thank all of the people who have helped me finish this latest project as well as those who have given me encouragement along the way. I never in my wildest dreams believed I would have actual fans, and now I have messages coming in from places like New Zealand, Great Britain, India, and Mexico. The support truly has been phenomenal.

I'd like to once more thank Derek Murphy of Creativindie Covers for creating another fantastic cover design, and the editors at Manuscript Magic for their excellent editing work.

Thank you to my friends and family for believing in me, thank you to my lovely wife, Kristin, and my boys, Kevin and Ryan, for keeping life interesting, and thank you to my parents for allowing me to watch gory zombie movies at an inappropriately young age.

Most importantly, thank you for taking an interest in my books. If you keep reading them, I'll keep writing them, and that's a promise.

Richard Johnson

Made in the USA
Middletown, DE
24 November 2015